My Wife's Black Boyfriend

By   I. M. Telling

Text Revision Date February 28, 2013

This material is intended for mature audiences only Warning: this story contains graphic descriptions of sexual content including sexual lust between a black man and a white woman.

Author's note: All characters depicted in this work of fiction are 18 years of age.

My Wife's Black Boyfriend

Hello friend,

I hope your day is going well. I received your email inquiry regarding my wife's black boyfriend, asking how we arrived at this place, and I just wanted to answer some of your questions. It has been quite a journey for sure, but getting there was definitely an enjoyable experience for both of us.

First off, I highly recommend that if your wife Tina does not have a black boyfriend yet, you really should help her pick one out, of course, the final decision on who she picks obviously needs to be hers. Does she have anyone on the short list yet? Giving her feedback on the ones you feel most comfortable with will help her make a decision.

My wife Connie has never been happier with hers, and it has added so much to our own relationship. I simply can't tell you how well this has worked out for her, for her boyfriend Jeremy, and for me as well.

I will start out by telling you how the three of us met. It started with an email that we received on one of the swinger sites we have a paid membership on called *SwingPartners*. Jeremy's online ID was **BullNBed**, which I thought was rather aggressive when I first saw it.

I was the one who logged in that day and when I saw that we had mail, I clicked on the mailbox icon to see what this black bull fellow had to say. I liked his initial message so much that I made a copy of it and saved it on the computer. Here is what it said.

Hello Robert and Connie

My name is Jeremy and I am new to this area although I am not new to this site. I have been in the lifestyle for many years. I hope this message finds both of you well.

Being new in the city, I wanted to begin making new friends and I came across your profile and liked what I saw. Connie, you are one of the most attractive women I have ever seen on this site and I would love to get to know you.

Your profile mentions that you occasionally enjoy meeting single males and, well I am single and I hope my profile generates some interest for you.

Although I have participated in threesomes with couples before, I prefer to enjoy a one on one time with the wife if possible. Robert, I hope this is something within your comfort and acceptability range.

Of course, many things happened before that email arrived in our inbox. Let me tell our story starting at the very beginning about how we arrived where we are today.

The first time we ever played, it was with one of Connie's friends from work. She had seen me a couple of times when I came to pick Connie up from work and well, I guess she must have liked what she saw because she started dropping hints to Connie. I'm still a little unsure of how subtle hints progressed to that evening when it was my thirtieth birthday.

I remember that period of time so well because for the first time, I wasn't seeing a young kid in the mirror when I shaved. What brought it home to me was that time about a year before when on a whim; I decided to let my beard grow out over the holidays when we spent two weeks visiting Connie's folks and mine. I'm one of those guys that started seeing a few gray hairs on his face at a young age. Believe me, that beard growth was gone a few minutes later. So far, the top hairs seem to be staying with me, no bald spots yet but I was beginning to sense that my hairline is on the move in a backward direction. My dad was bald at forty so, I worry about that a lot.

Connie called me at work that day and asked me if I'd stop by the bakery and pick up my cake. I remember thinking at the time that wasn't that something she was supposed to do for me? Well, I told her I would but I was a little miffed that she had asked me to and I suppose it came out in my voice. However, then she said, "Honey, I would have picked it up for you but I've been busy setting up your surprise."

Well, that made me feel better, after all, everyone likes surprises. I asked her, "What is it?" and she just replied, "You'll see."

So, try to imagine this if you can. I walked in carrying that cake and Connie tells me to wait in the living room while she heads down the hallway towards our bedroom, telling me that she is going to light the candles. I was supposed to come in to the bedroom when she called me after everything was setup. She said, "Your surprise will be ready for you in a few minutes, now don't peek!"

I sat down and lit up a cigarette but before I could finish half of it, I heard Connie calling my name and telling me to come in. I had no idea what delicious pleasures lay ahead of me that night. I walked down the hallway to the bedroom and opened the door. I had not expected that it was going to be totally dark inside the bedroom so I didn't flip on the hallway light, the only light was coming in was from the living room far down the hallway and the candles on the cake.

All I could see at first was the glow from the candles; all thirty of them, as they flickered and cast shadows in the room, and Connie sitting in the middle of the bed holding the cake and I could see that she was naked. That was when I realized it, that it was not my wife Connie sitting on the bed, holding that cake out before me.

As I realized that it was another woman, I heard Connie's voice coming from the back corner of the bedroom saying, "Robert, this is my friend Denise from work. She wants to help me give you your birthday present."

With Denise already naked, it was an easy leap for me to figure out what they had planned for me. The funny thing is that Connie and I had never even talked about any kind of open marriage or sex with others before that night. In fact, we had never really talked much about our experiences before we got married other than we both knew we had been with other people. So obviously, this was a real surprise to say the least.

If my teeth could glow, I would have illuminated the entire room with my smile. Everybody hears stories like this but I never thought it would happen to me. I walked over to the bed and blew out the candles, which was a mistake because that really made the room black inside. I took the cake from Denise, getting icing all over my fingers, as I took it from her and placed it on the dresser.

I tasted the icing on my hand as I walked back towards the bed and naked Denise, but I wasn't licking my lips because of the icing. I was definitely ready to taste my birthday present. I sat down beside her and she and I started kissing each other. It is so strange to meet a woman for the first time when she is naked. We stopped kissing briefly while she whispered, "Happy Birthday Robert," in my ear; even her voice aroused me, it was so sexy.

Of course, I was well aware that Connie was watching us, as I quickly pulled off my shirt and pants. I was already hard by the time I climbed back onto the bed. Funny, but if someone would have asked me if I would have been self-conscious to have someone watching me having sex, I'm sure I would have said that I probably wouldn't have been able to perform. You just never know do you?

The first time I came that night with Denise was orally. She took total charge and made me lay down flat on my back while she went down on me. I hate to admit it but later, I felt I had to lie to Connie about how good Denise was at sucking cock but, since that night, Connie has had a lot of practice and I'd match her skills against anyone and she is just as good at it now as Denise is, and probably better.

I really love it when a woman begs me to shoot cum in her mouth and it's extra special when the woman swallows, rather than spitting it back out on you or into a napkin. I really feel that the act of consuming a man's seed is one thing that a woman can do for a man that really has her giving herself to her partner. I really pity men whose wives won't do that for them. Don't those wives ever stop to think or realize that there are other women available to their husbands who will?

After I came that first time in her mouth, Denise and I were lying on the bed together and Connie came over and sat down next to us. Now, at this point in the evening, Connie still had all her clothes on. Since this was my surprise party, I think her original plan was just to let me enjoy Denise one-on-one.

Since it had been over six years since I had been with another woman besides Connie, it didn't take me long before I was able to rise to the occasion (drum roll please). This time, I wanted my cock buried inside of Denise's pussy… that was something that I was going to insist on. The only problem however, was that I did not have any condoms. I asked Connie, "Did you happen to think about picking up any condoms?"

It was Denise that whispered, "Baby, you don't need one with me, I'd rather you didn't use one anyway. I like having a man cum inside me."

Wow, I thought, I had never had a woman say anything like that to me before. The thing is, I hate the damn things myself, maybe because it just seems to interrupt the flow, pardon the pun. Taking the time to stop what you are doing, find one, get it open and then rolled out can kill the moment, at least that is the way it is for me.

I turned and looked at Connie to see what she thought and she blew me away when she said, "I don't like them either. It feels so much better when the man fills you up. It really makes you feel like a woman."

I remember having a few fleeting images when she said that, of hardened clay vessels, being filed with the essence of a man while the jars symbolized the woman. I had never experienced thoughts such as this before, and as a man, I just looked at the whole fluids issue as being wet and messy. After what Denise and Connie had said, I actually felt it was my duty as a man to fill Denise's *vessel* with every drop of semen my nuts could create.

With Connie's continued support and approval, I was on Denise like there was no tomorrow. We began again by kissing passionately and open mouthed, playing tongue tag with each other but this time, I reached down and started getting my fingers wet. Denise was already flowing from the excitement, possibly even before I had entered the room. To this day, I still wish I could have listened in when Connie and Denise first started talking and planning this surprise party for me.

The first time I fucked Denise, Connie was just sitting on the edge of the bed watching us as we played. Since I had already come once that evening, I was having a few issues, I couldn't get off, and I was having a little trouble with it going a little soft on me. Regardless, we played then stopped for a few moments, just kissing and massaging each other, and then fucked a little more. The evening was very relaxed with nothing rushed. It was during one of the just touching periods when Connie added her hands to the mix as well and at Denise and my urging, soon Connie was naked too.

Most men dream about being with two hot, great looking women at the same time. I had no idea if this was my one and only chance or something that might happen occasionally. It was so much fun because we all acted like little kids on a playground. It felt so naughty.

Finally, maybe just after eleven that night, we were all so tired that we gave out and just laid there on the bed, with me in the middle of the two girls. Denise said, "It's getting late, maybe we should cut the cake because Rodney is going to start wondering where I am."

"I said, "Rodney?"

"Rodney is my husband."

Despite the fact that I had just committed adultery myself, the idea that Denise was married came as a shock. All of a sudden, I was worried that maybe her husband might find out and want to beat my head in or something.

I even stuttered when I asked, "What time were you supposed to be home?"

"I told him it would be late by the time we got finished, so we're not *that* rushed; he knows where I am and what I'm doing."

"He… does?"

Denise said, "Relax, Baby, we've been swingers for nearly two years now."

As I heard that word Denise had used, *swingers*, it dawned on me that although I knew what the word meant; I guess I wasn't really sure people actually did that, that it was more of an urban myth or something. She just seemed so nonchalant about it all that I wasn't sure what to think.

"I'm sure Rodney would love to get with Connie sometime," remarked Denise, "and she'd enjoy him too."

It's funny, a few moments earlier although I didn't know it at the time, I was fucking another man's wife. As amazing as that was at the time, it just seemed like a lot of fun and no big thing but when Denise brought up the subject of her husband Rodney being with Connie, it was like cold water splashing in my face. I really didn't know what to say. I heard myself saying, "Yeah sure, bet she would," but that wasn't what I was thinking.

I looked over at Connie and she had the same look I might have expected to see if the three of us were just talking about a future night out, like a double date to go to a restaurant for dinner. There was no discernible reaction at all on Connie's face as we chatted about her fucking another man. Weird, huh?

"Let's eat some cake!" said Denise.

"Yes," said Connie, and without bothering to put on a robe or anything, she walked out of the room to get plates. Denise and I didn't say anything while she was out, we just kept touching each other, not really a massage kind of thing, more like an exploration and I was really enjoying just doing that.

Connie came back in a few minutes later with three saucers, three forks, and three glasses of milk. The cake was cut and we three all enjoyed a slice as we sat in a triangle on our bed, completely naked, au natural.

Soon after we finished our cake slices, Denise started putting her clothes back on. I just sat back and watched as she did it and even that was fun. Connie escorted Denise to the front door and I heard Denise urging Connie to give Rodney a call. I heard Connie agreeing that she would.

It was a little awkward after Denise left, with just Connie and I. She said, "I hope you enjoyed your birthday surprise," and I assured her I did but little else was said that night. We were both exhausted and it was another workday coming the next morning. I slept sounder than I had in years that night.

The next morning, neither of us mentioned anything about what had occurred the night before. I couldn't help notice that I was still naked when I woke up, and additional evidence from the previous night's party was visible on the nightstand; three saucers, three forks, and three empty milk glasses. My clothes and Connie's were still lying on the floor next to the bed.

It was two days later while Connie and I were out to dinner one night when Connie casually mentioned that she had called Rodney and chatted with him. In hindsight, that was the best place she could have chosen to bring it up because being in a public place, I forced myself to stay calm and reserved.

It was a real quandary for me. How could I say no after what had already happened? Moreover, to be honest, I did not know if I wanted to say no. That night with Denise in our bed had been almost a magical experience. I will always remember that moment when I realized that the naked woman holding that cake with thirty candles wasn't Connie.

"Oh," I said, as I stabbed my backed potato.

"Yes, he seems really nice. I already feel like I know him."

Subconsciously, I was already applying a biblical reference to *know him*. The thought excited me as images began to form of what it would look like to see Connie with another man on top of her.

"They've asked us if we'd like to come over to their house Saturday night."

"What did you say," I asked her, trying to remain emotionless. I don't know why I felt I needed to be so reserved about it; of course the truth is that I already knew I wanted it to happen. I also felt that I shouldn't want it to happen but I kept telling myself that if I had issues about this sort of thing, I should have said so before letting Denise suck my cock.

I asked, "What did you tell him?"

"I said I'd need to check with you, but it would probably be all right."

I just nodded silently because that was so much easier than talking about it. I'll be truthful here and tell you that in the back of my mind, I started wondering if Connie was more experienced at this adultery thing than she let on. I began to build scenarios in my head where she was fucking different men all over town behind my back. Crazy as that sounds, that also excited me.

I didn't really believe she had been unfaithful with me, but all this seemed to be such a normal thing for her. Obviously, she could adapt to changing environments a lot quicker than I was able to. She made it even clearer to me when upon seeing me nod my head, she responded with, "Good."

Not another word was mentioned regarding Saturday night until Saturday night arrived. At around six o'clock, we both simply started getting ready to go out for the evening.

I felt I needed a little liquid courage so once dressed, I asked Connie if she'd like a drink.

"You read my mind," she said, "Are you nervous?"

I made the drinks doubles. "Ya think?" I quipped. I handed one of the highball glasses to Connie. "Are you sure you're up for this?" I asked.

"It's a little late to ask, don't you think?" she replied.

"It's earlier than later will be," I countered.

"True," she murmured.

"So, what do you think?" I asked.

"Well, what I think is… that this is kind of unfair to you," she said.

I asked, "How so?"

"Well, I mean… well,"

I stood there with my bourbon and water, mostly bourbon and waited on her to tell me what was on her mind.

"I don't know, I guess it's because I've already been there."

"You mean, with Rodney?"

"Oh no… that's not what I meant, not at all. Honey, I've never cheated on you and, well I *never* will! I don't consider this cheating. Do you? I meant I was there when you did it with Denise. I saw you having sex with another woman so, I already know how it feels. But you, you have never been on the other side of this, watching me with another man. Do you think you can handle it okay?"

"I don't know," I said. What else could I say and still give her an honest answer. I had no illusions that Connie wanted to go forward with this, and for the most part, I was excited about it as well but a man never really knows which of his heads is doing the thinking.

After reflecting for a moment, I told her, "I think we need to find out if this is something we want, and I don't think we can truly know that unless we try it and see. What I can promise is, that I will try to be okay, but if either of us starts having second thoughts, then we walk away from it right then."

"I agree," Connie said, "and, no repercussions if this blows up on us."

I also agreed with what Connie said about repercussions, but even before we walked out our front door, I was already aware that my wife wanted to have sex with another man. That train had already left the station. What if we actually started playing and Rodney has his dick inside Connie, what if that's when I lose it? You can't un-fuck someone, one dick, one pussy, once they are connected, that's fucking.

Twenty-five minutes later, we were on Denise and Rodney's front porch. I'm not sure who was more nervous, Connie or me, but once I pressed that doorbell button; we both knew that we would be testing the strength of our relationship as never before.

Both Denise and Rodney came to the door. I had worried that they might both already be naked and I didn't think I was ready

15

for that. However, greetings were exchanged, and they invited us into their home just as if everything seemed normal, but of course, things were not normal. Rodney immediately suggested that he should fix everyone a round of drinks.

On the drive over, I could not put aside the realization that Connie and me were going to Denise and Rodney's house to fuck and be fucked. The thought of being with Denise again appealed to me and I tried to focus on that rather than think about my wife being with another man. I kept telling myself that there had been other people we were with before we were married. I had never had any issues knowing that Connie had been with other men before, and that as long as everything was in the open, this shouldn't make any difference either.

Naturally, we instantly paired off, as Denise escorted me to the living room couch while Connie assisted Rodney with his bartender duties. Their home was very neat; everything looked to be in its proper place, nothing garish or unpleasant with the furnishings or decorations. In addition to the sofa and a large chair, the room also contained a love seat, with all three of the pieces forming a nice pit group.

There was an extremely deep-pile floor carpet in the center of the room. I could not help but imagine how four people might use that rug as a play area, as I remembered Denise's admission that her and her husband had been swingers for two years. Was it just two years or over two years? Somehow, that seemed important to me at that moment, perhaps because I thought it might improve the accuracy of any guesses I might make on how many people had fucked on that rug.

Connie handed Denise and I our glasses and then she sat down on the love seat next to Rodney, her feet pulled up onto the cushions as she kicked off her shoes. Denise was already barefoot. Everyone seems to be getting comfortable I thought.

There were a few initial moments of awkward conversation, as Rodney and I tried to get to know each other but then things moved quickly when Rodney asked me if I had enjoyed my birthday present. I remembered thinking, how do you tell a man that you enjoyed fucking his wife?

"It a… it was, rather nice actually," I stammered.

"Denise said she thought you enjoyed it," remarked Rodney. "She's mentioned her interest in you for a while now; she just didn't know whether you and Connie were open to something."

"I see," I said, "but… so, how did she know? I mean, I didn't really ask Connie how all this came up."

"Well," Rodney laughed, "I guess it takes one to know one."

I wasn't sure how to respond to that. For a moment, I began to wonder about how flirtatious Connie might be around the people she worked with.

Connie spoke up, "We just started talking over lunch one day, and well, one thing led to another."

"I see," I said again, wondering if I was being too naïve about everything. "So, how long… how did you and Denise get into this… this open marriage stuff?"

"It's how we met," answered Rodney. "I was at a swinger's party with another lady friend, and Denise was there with a guy friend she knew. It's funny; we didn't even know what each other's name was the first time we fucked."

Well friend, I don't want to bore you with all the details, but it wasn't long before all four of us were down on that carpet fucking and sucking like crazy. Denise started things off by reaching over and pulling at my belt. I wasn't watching Connie that closely at that moment but I believe it was Rodney who made the first move, pulling Connie over close to him and then kissing her. I glanced up just as Rodney was reaching inside Connie's blouse the first time but then Denise demanded my attention and I focused on the woman I was with at that moment.

Denise and Rodney introduced us to some of their other friends and we started going to house parties and meeting other couples. One of the things I learned immediately about myself is that I really enjoyed seeing Connie getting fucked. I guess there is a lot of voyeur in me. Connie learned that she is also quite the exhibitionist. That's really how her having a black boyfriend came about, but I'm getting ahead of my story here.

Since I liked watching, we started to occasionally meet with single guys and have threesomes. Sometimes, I would not even participate, I would just sit back and enjoy the show and Connie enjoyed that too, me watching her.

I guess it was a year ago when some guy on this site emailed us and asked if it would be possible for Connie to be his 'date' at a couples only party that he wanted to attend. Well, at first, we were going to turn him down but we ended up giving him permission after he came over to the house one evening.

He wasn't really Connie's type but she played with him anyway because he was such a pleasant fellow, just real shy and reserved. I suspect that the man didn't get lucky that often, people tend to put so much into someone's appearance, even more so within the lifestyle, despite the fact that there are very few Ken and Barbies out there.

As I said, we came close to just sending him a polite no but Connie was curious about why he couldn't find his own date so she talked me into letting him come over. To be honest, she had to seduce him or nothing would have happened. I remembered thinking that perhaps, Connie was damn near the first woman he had ever been with. The idea of this man at a full-blown sex orgy party was hard to visualize.

After he left that night, I assumed that we would never see him again but Connie said she didn't have a problem with being his 'date' to a party. She said, "We're just going to walk in together, we will each do our own thing, and then leave together when the party is over."

I guess I just felt that, well, that it was a nice thing for her to do for him and I told her that I agreed with her and that I thought she should do it for him. We called him together and my God, I think he must have been masturbating on the other end of the line.

I guess it was one hell of a party that night too. Connie told me she did it with five different men that night, and the guy she went with, he ended up having a threesome with two women, lucky guy.

It was when Connie was telling me about her experiences at the party that I realized how much I enjoyed hearing her talk about it. When we went to parties together, we just did our thing and afterwards, on the way home we usually talked about other things, you know, normal stuff such as deferred home maintenance, job stuff, and possible vacation spots. Hearing Connie go into all those details about the party she had attended was different and I liked listening to her narrative.

Anyway, what happened next is that the guy she went with was so grateful that Connie had gone as his 'date' that he emailed us asking if he could take Connie out for a nice dinner; a real 'date' date to thank her with steak and lobster. It was my idea that she accepted his offer.

So, try to picture this, it was a Friday night, Joey, which was his name, he came to pick her up. Connie was still putting on her final makeup touches so I answered the door, asked him in, and offered him a drink. It was the weirdest feeling, as if I was Connie's Daddy and this Joey guy was coming to take her to the Prom. I had to force myself to not tell him that I expected him to have her home before curfew while pointing a stern eyeball towards him.

Connie, finally done with her primping, comes out into the living room and a few minutes later, the two of them leave. I grabbed the remote, sat down, and flipped around on the channels until I found something to watch but my mind kept wondering what they were doing.

This was like watching, except I was watching with my mind, not with my eyes, I fantasized everything. I'm not saying this was better than sitting back and watching Connie getting

20

pounded on, but it put things in an entirely different perspective; not better, not worse, just different but still rather pleasurable. The mind really is your most active sex organ, I remember reading that somewhere.

I had all these images playing out like a movie in my head, from him opening her car door to her holding his hand while they drove to the restaurant. In my fantasy, I saw them using valet parking, which I knew was unlikely however there they were. The other people in the restaurant, none of them knew or suspected that Joey was out with a married woman. It almost seemed like some crazy prank that we, all three of us, were playing on the rest of the world. We three had a secret and I remembered thinking that I hoped Connie would ham it up some, so that casual onlookers would be convinced that there was something going on between her and her date.

As it got later in the evening, I started getting tired and I wondered if I could sleep while Connie was out on her date. Even the word *date* seemed to excite me in some strange way. I kept saying to myself, "My wife is out on a date!" To be honest, I was surprised that I was able to fall asleep so easily that night and as my little fantasy sort of morphed into my dreams.

One thing I did that night was to go to bed in the spare bedroom. This seemed to play into my fantasy, that if Joey and Connie came back to play, that she should have the master bedroom. I'm not sure when they finally got home that night, but I don't think it was very late.

When I first woke up the next morning, I immediately hopped out of bed and went out into the hallway to see if Connie was back and if she had company. Our bedroom door was never normally closed around our house but it was closed that morning so I assumed she had company. A quick peek out to the driveway confirmed it. Funny thing was Joey's car looked exactly how I had fantasized it to be. It was the same color, same style, not sure about the make, model, or year because these days, who can tell anyway?

I tried to be quiet so as not to disturb them. I made the coffee and was just pouring my first cup when Connie strolled into the kitchen. She was just wearing her robe. I could not tell for sure but I suspected that the robe was all she was wearing. Neither of us acted as if anything was unusual or out of the ordinary.

Perhaps ten minutes later, Joey came into the kitchen but he was already dressed. Even with him sitting at the breakfast table with us, both Connie and I wearing our robes, no one spoke about what had transpired since he and Connie had left over ten hours earlier on their date.

I don't mean to get all-philosophical on you, friend; but as I retell these events I realize that I continue to make the claim that everything seemed so normal and natural. I was fucking other women and my wife was fucking other men. She had entertained a man in *our* bedroom while I slept in the guest room. The real point of everything I have and will continue to relate to you is that our relationship, the union of Connie and Robert had always remained the constant and never changing aspect of what we do. She and I love each other and we have trust in ways most people can never fathom. With that base and foundation, regardless of what transpired, we really were at ease with everything.

Back to the story, after Joey left, Connie spent over an hour going over every detail of what had transpired while I waited at home and then additional juicy details about what went down while I was sleeping. I was so aroused listening to Connie tell me all her 'secrets' that I couldn't resist myself and I pulled her into the bedroom and fucked her on the same sheets Joey had fucked her on that night. There was even a damp spot, which I think was Joey's semen on the sheets.

That first date wound up being just the first of many that followed. Joey really was her first *boyfriend* although she never became romantically involved with him. They just went out occasionally, sometime to dinner, sometime to a movie, sometimes both, and then he would bring her home and they would spend the night together. I always made my bed in the guest bedroom when Joey stayed over.

One thing I found interesting is that I no longer needed Connie to tell me everything that happened while she was out with Joey. My imagined story was enough to satisfy me all by itself although each new tidbit allowed me to create visions with greater depth and story. Maybe I am simply having sex with myself using mental masturbation. Regardless, it was working for me and also, Connie loved the sense of personal freedom that this seemed to bring to her life.

The *affair*, and isn't that a deliciously wicked word, ended when Joey's job transferred him across country about four months after we first met him. I remember that Connie became teary-eyed that last night when they were together and I realized that she had built up an emotional connection with Joey after all. The amazing thing was, that I didn't feel the least bit jealous of that fact. I guess it reinforced to us both just how strong our own relationship was that her falling in love to some extent with another man did not threaten *us* and never could or would.

With Joey gone, Connie and I continued doing what we had done before he came along by attending parties and meeting couples, not that we actually stopped of course. However, there were evenings when there wasn't a party going on somewhere that I sensed that Connie was longing to have those single-girl experiences that she had enjoyed being Joey's *girlfriend*. I suggested to her that we change our online profile to indicate that *wife enjoys being treated as a single girl, asked out, and dated.* Connie was against the idea at first, saying that it would lead to being buried by single men wanting to get with her. I quipped back to her, "And, so?"

That's what happened too. There were probably three times as many first contacts from single men as there were couples. Sometimes, Connie would get phone calls two and three times a day from one of her guy friends. Sometimes they would ask her out, sometimes it was just to chat.

Many of the guys just wanted to come over and fuck rather than put out the effort to take her out for the evening. Although Connie often did fuck those men, she favored the ones who wanted more than just to come over for a quick fuck.

Sometimes I'd watch or join in, sometimes not. I actually thought it was somewhat funny to keep Connie in suspense regarding my degree of involvement on a given night.

Her dating also lead to overnights away from home occasionally, and a few times for extended weekend trips to the beach. Connie always made sure however, that she relayed as much information about those away times that I seemed to need.

So, by now, I suppose you're asking about how this black thing started, right? Well, it wasn't really any different except that one day, for the first time, the guy sending her an email about meeting was an African American. She turned him down, initially anyway.

Normally, it would be me that would log into the *SwingPartners* web site to check for messages and search for couples that I thought we might like to meet with. If there was new mail and the email was a single guy wanting to meet or possibly date Connie, I'd call her over and let her do the correspondence. One afternoon, an email came in and as I usually did, I clicked on his profile to see what it had to say about him. I was knocked over the first time the profile picture showed a black man.

My reaction was like, whoa… what the fuck? If I had been standing up, I swear to you that I would have stepped backwards, as if I had been walking along and came face to face with a big spider. Once I got over my initial shock, I started reading his profile. If I had not seen his black face in his profile picture, I would have assumed that he was white just like us.

I started to ignore his email but then I got to thinking about what Connie would do if she knew a black man was interested in her. I had never asked her if she had been with a black man, although I was sure that by now, it would have come out if she

25

had. You know what they say about curiosity, I had to know what Connie's reaction would be.

I re-read his profile, every word of it at least three times. The emails we usually received from single men focused on either the dating/single girl stuff, possible interest in a threesome, or down and dirty can we fuck messages. This message appeared somewhere between the *threesome* and *let's fuck* type. It read simply, "Let's meet for some adult fun," and it wasn't specific about whether he just wanted to meet Connie or whether he wanted to meet us both.

Trying to sound as normal as possible, I called out, "Connie, you got an email from a guy on *SwingPartners*."

"Okay, give me a minute. Who is it?"

I replied, "Just some new guy," and I closed out his profile and left it on the screen that showed all of our incoming emails. A few minutes later, Connie walked in and I could hear her click the mouse to read the message and then another click, which I assumed, meant she was looking at his profile. I maintained my nonchalant attitude; waiting to hear what she would say when she saw that the guy was black.

She didn't say a word but I heard her as she typed out a message to him. A few moments later, the clicking stopped and I could visualize her re-reading her own words before she hit the send key. CLICK.

Still waiting to hear her comments, I continued holding the magazine I had hastily grabbed when I first sat down. I chuckled when I noticed that I was holding it open upside down. Connie didn't say a word. She just got up and headed back towards the bedroom hallway.

I had to ask before she was out of earshot, "So, what did you tell him?"

She stopped for a second, and then turned around and walked into the living room. She had a very serious look on her face.

"I told him I only met people of my own race."

"Okay," I said, trying to show no concerns or interest either way, and frankly, I thought that would be the end of it. I went back over to the computer because originally, I had intended on looking around to see if any of our couple's friends were online and might want to get together that evening.

Twice, I interrupted my searches to go back and look at the black man's profile. Although I believed that Connie had told him exactly what she told me she had written, I clicked on the link to show sent mail messages. The words were exactly what Connie had said she had written. Again, I thought this would be the end of it and, seeing nothing else that interested me at the moment, I went back into the kitchen to load the morning's breakfast dishes into the dishwasher.

I couldn't get this black man thing out of my mind. Truthfully, I didn't know how I felt about it. Part of me was upset, mad even; put off by the whole idea of a black man being interested in my wife.

I wasn't raised prejudiced but over the years you pick up a few, well, opinions from other people around you. Most of the people I worked with, and earlier at school, they were all white and some of these people did grow up in families where racial prejudice was practiced. That shit can rub off on you in subtle ways and then there is the taboo factor itself.

On the other hand, a fantasy was taking shape and frankly, I began to crave the idea of seeing Connie with a black man.

The rest of the morning, I was plagued by memories of his profile picture and continued fantasies as well as those initial repulsions I had experienced. I knew one thing and that was that the fantasies were winning. I was afraid that over the course of that morning, I was becoming obsessed with the idea of Connie crossing the color line and having sex with a black man.

Being born in the early eighties, I'm not sure why I was so enthralled about the taboo aspects of it but I knew that was a part of it. One of my most recurring fantasies when Connie was out on one of her dates was the whole perception thing by those other people who were sitting at surrounding dinner tables in the restaurant or the people behind Connie and her date in line at the movie theater to buy tickets. What if the guy she was with was a black man? I hated to admit it, but anytime I happened to notice a black man and a white woman together, I automatically jumped to the conclusion that sex was involved.

Since Connie had already displayed her feelings about interracial when she had told him in her email reply that she preferred to stay with her own race, by lunchtime I was starting to put the whole thing aside but it would not remain there, dismissed for long.

We were having lunch, ham sandwiches and for some reason, I will always remember what we were eating that day. Connie started off with, "What did you think about that email we got?"

"You mean, on *SwingPartners* this morning?" I asked, as if I didn't know exactly what she was talking about.

"Yes."

"I dunno," I mumbled, trying to act calmly about it and hiding that fact that I was fucking pissing my pants to see where this would go. "Just a guy I guess, why?"

"Were you surprised?" she asked.

Well, as they saying goes, the camel's nose was inside the tent and also they say you can't ignore the elephant in the room either so I said, "You mean because he was black?"

Connie looked at me and although she didn't say it, I heard her words clearly, "Of course because he's black you fucking idiot!"

Seeing that Connie was waiting on me to continue, I said, "Well, unusual I guess. How do you feel about it?"

Connie asked, "You mean meeting him?"

I'm trying to relay to you friend, just what was going through my mind just then. When Connie said what she said, using the words *meeting him*, it hit me in the strangest way. The best way I can describe how I felt is to use an analogy.

Imagine for a moment that you are one of those little tokens they use in a Monopoly game, and the other player, my wife in this case, is going around the board about as fast as I was but we were still both a lot closer to the beginning of the board than the end where you pass GO and receive two hundred dollars. Well, it was her turn to follow the roll of the dice and she lands on one of those chance or community chest squares and the card reads, "Advance to Boardwalk".

She wasn't just counting out steps, her token was whizzing around the board, passing all my houses and hotels and landing on Boardwalk and she could buy it from the bank if she wanted. This was a game changer and it all happened in the blink of an eye; the words m*eeting him,* with *him* being a black man, had been spoken aloud.

Of course, actually meeting was not what she had suggested but it was immediately clear to me that Connie had some interest because, why else would she have brought it back up.

"It's… certainly something different," I allowed.

"I think we should," Connie said flatly.

I did not agree, at least on principle, but also, I was thinking with that little head and I knew it. My fantasies were going berserk and before I could stop myself, I replied, "If you want to," but then my big head, the one on top my shoulders added, "if you're sure you can handle it."

I wondered, whom am I asking? Everything your typical white man thinks about as far as black men and white women was blazing afire in my brain. Handling it meant the entire gauntlet between the psychologically as well as the physically. Visions of huge big black cocks hanging down around the knees on black bucks were crystal clear in my head and once you go black reverberated in my ears. Would she feel degraded? Would I? I told myself that black men were just men but still, this was crossing a *line*. I laughed when I thought of the idea of a *color line*.

"So, you're okay with it?" she asked.

I didn't really feel I had a choice, "I am if you are," I said.

"Fine," Connie smiled, in an almost contented fashion.

I sat there at the kitchen table and continued eating my ham sandwich. I wondered what thoughts Connie must have had while she was doing her morning chores while I was having my own interracial fantasies.

I made the obvious comment, "But you already told him we didn't meet black guys."

"We'll send him another email, telling him we reconsidered." She said.

"Okay," I said, "now?"

"Yes," she said, "let's send it together."

"Okay."

We both got up from the table and walked towards the small desk where the computer was and Connie sat down while I just stood behind her. I was glad that she had volunteered to type the message. I watched as she typed it out.

"Dear Sir,

Please disregard our previous email. We have reconsidered your request to meet and have decided that yes, we would enjoy meeting you."

She signed it Connie and Robert, and, after proofing it once, she hit the send key. We both sat there, as if expecting an immediate response. I know we were both disappointed when three minutes passed and there was no new message. However, about an hour later, we received a response, the only thing the message contained was a phone number.

I remember that it was Connie that was logging on and rechecking that day, about every fifteen minutes or so. I remember how I had been so surprised to see her this keen to get a response. As we saw the number, Connie said, "Should I call?"

I wanted to say something smartass about, "That's what you've been checking for every fifteen minutes," but I just replied. "Sure."

Connie picked up the house phone and started dialing after glancing back at the computer screen one last time to get number. It went to voice mail and Connie identified herself and left our number. I wouldn't be exaggerating to say that we were both disappointed.

I wanted to say, "Connie, let's talk about this a little more." But before I could speak, the phone started ringing. Connie and I both looked at each other for a brief moment before she picked up the phone and said hello.

I listened to Connie's side of the call and obviously, the man at the other end was pushing her about meeting. Frankly, if he had been a white man, I suspect Connie would have brushed him off, "Well, nice talking to you." A few minutes later, Connie gave him our address.

"His name is Franklin but he says to call him Frank, he sounds okay I guess. I told him he could come over. What have I done?"

No, she didn't say, "What have I done," but yes, she had told him he could come to meet us. I do believe we both shared some of the same misgivings.

"When is he supposed to get here?" I asked.

"He said he's leaving now?"

"Now?"

"Yeah, he said he should be here in less than half an hour," Connie said. "Oh my, I'm a mess."

I didn't think she was a mess, but before I could say anything she was headed back towards the bedroom I assumed to take a quick shower and get dressed. She yelled back over her shoulder, "Straighten up the living room."

I looked around, straightened one of the sofa pillows up and picked up the magazine I had pretended to read earlier that morning when Connie first saw his email. Once the magazine was safely hidden from view, I sat down in my easy chair to wait.

I remembered that night long before when Connie and I were just about to leave to go over and 'fuck' Denise and Rodney and tried to equate this current situation to that one.

Unfortunately, it was far too early in the day for me to pour myself a drink but then I gave into my urges and poured one although just a single shot. I wondered if I should mix one for Connie but decided to leave her alone while she did her own preparations.

Perhaps the one thing I most wondered was whether a new thing would have been added to our list of experiences by evening. I assumed there would be. As I waited on either Connie to return to the living room or for the doorbell to ring, I tried to use my imagination to picture what it would look like to see Connie with a black man and despite everything I had seen before, I couldn't get it to materialize for me. This was just too different.

Twenty minutes passed and Connie returned to the room. She sat down on the sofa and we both continued out wait. I wished that Connie had waited until the man got here, so I could have reached some sort of comfort level with the man myself first. Having her sitting a few feet away from me on the couch fidgeting was making me even more nervous than I already was.

She hadn't overdone it with her attire and I was please to see her in clothing that would have worked nicely for a trip to the grocery store. We continued to wait and I checked my wristwatch and saw that thirty-five minutes had passed since Connie had declared that he was due in thirty. Five minutes wasn't late but those five seemed like fifty.

Five more minutes passed as we sat in the living room waiting. I got up to fix myself another drink and asked Connie if she would like one also.

"No, wait and see what our company wants to do," she said. Five more minutes passed making him ten minutes late. Tick, tick, tick.

"Should we call him? To see if he got lost?" I ventured.

"No, I'm sure he's just running late," Connie declared, although she wasn't very convincing. No-shows had occasionally victimized most of our friends in the lifestyle but no matter how many times it happens, you always hope this time won't be one of them.

This time was different. This time, we were possibly crossing another line. I couldn't help but wonder whether a no-show from this man, whose name I had already forgotten, was happening. If he did turn out to be a no-show, would that be the end of the idea of Connie going black? I thought that might very well be the case.

At the fifty-minute mark, I saw light reflections on the wall that told me that someone might have pulled into our driveway. I got up to see and sure enough, a dark blue Subaru was there and I could see the man getting out of the car.

I probably looked funny as I tried to decide whether to wait for the bell to ring or just open the door on my own. "What's his name again?"

"Franklyn... Frank," Connie said.

"Right," and I made the decision to walk towards the front door. The bell rang just as I turned the knob. I remember seeing a big grin on his face, as if he expected to get some white pussy any minute.

"Welcome to our home," I said, which was my customary greeting to a single man who was coming to meet with Connie.

"Thanks man," Frank said, as he walked it. I saw him immediately looking towards Connie and his grin became wider. I knew he was sure he was about to get some off Connie. I still wasn't sure myself, nor at all sure whether I wanted him to or not.

I suppose that there are people out there, probably younger ones however, who don't see the color of another person's skin any more importantly that they observe the color of someone's shirt or blouse. I wish I was that way but I'm not and I knew Connie also had, well not issues, but still something that segregated her or kept her apart and with her own race. Yet I also knew that for me, there was an excitement here, this breaking of taboos or going where others don't. It attracted me and repelled me at the same time.

"How are you Pretty Lady?" Frank said to Connie.

"I'm fine, and how are you?" she replied.

"Come in and sit down," I said.

"Yes, I'd love to," he said. Together, we walked into the center of the room and Frank took a seat beside Connie on the couch. I returned to my easy chair.

"So, how long have you been on *SwingPartners*?" I asked.

"Not long, a couple of months," he replied, but he was speaking to Connie. I almost felt invisible in the room. I felt I wanted to push things into the obvious so I asked, "Have you met many white couples on there?"

"A few," he said, as he placed his hand on Connie's knee. She ignored it at first, but then she took his hand with hers. I knew this was a good sign, or rather an indication that she was willing to see where things would go. It being a good sign was a question I assumed wouldn't be answered until afterwards.

"Can I fix you a drink?" I asked.

"Yeah, if the lady would have one with me," he said, his eyes locked on Connie's breast,

"Connie?" I asked.

"Ah, yeah, do we still have any wine left?"

"I think so, in the fridge. Frank?"

"Yeah," he said.

I got up and walked into the kitchen. We had opened a bottle of white zinfandel the night before, and considering that I rarely allowed wine to stay in the bottle once I had opened it, last night had been an exception. I looked inside and the bottle was still about a third full. After grabbing a couple of wine glasses out of the pantry, I filled them and saw that there was still a little remaining in the bottle. I quickly downed it.

By the time I returned to the living room, Connie and Frank were wrapped in each other's arms kissing. It, well it shocked me to see it happening. I was in a state of shock, my mind overloaded by the imagery I was witnessing.

I set the two wine glasses on the coffee table near them quietly and then grabbed my highball glass and went back to the kitchen to refresh it. It would be my third of the early afternoon. I glanced at the clock on the stove and it read one-fifteen. This time, I poured a double from the bottle of Jim Beam, noticing that it was only half-full now. I added just a dash more bourbon to my glass, which left little room for the coke I intended to mix with it.

Seeing Connie with Rodney that first night had been etched in my memory like stone but this was something else altogether. The few seconds I had been in the living room while Connie kissed back as aggressively as Frank was kissing her was etched in steel, and would remain in my memory for the rest of my life, whether I wanted to remember or not. All I knew was that those first few seconds was enough for a first look.

I took a drink from my glass and then grabbed the bottle of Jim Beam and added another shot to it. I was beginning to feel the alcohol as it flowed through my blood system. Ready for another view, I headed back into the living room.

The activity underway on the sofa was not too different now than it had been a few minutes earlier although now Frank's hand was inside Connie's blouse and her hand was grasping at what Frank had growing in his pants. I sat down quietly to watch. I wanted to say something like, "Guess you guys are getting to know each other," or asking, "You two having fun?" but I remained silent.

The level of intensity between Frank and Connie couldn't remain at this level for long that was the one thing I knew for sure. I wondered if they would fuck on the couch and that made me glance around the room to see if all the curtains were drawn.

Connie and I had often wondered if our neighbors had noticed how often we went out these days, or how often we had company stopping by, especially when a strange car remained in our driveway until morning. When I was growing up, I lived in a neighborhood similar to the one where Connie and I live today, as she had as well, but back then, I knew all of our neighbors really well. I know I would have noticed all the 'goings-on', but Connie and I had never really gotten to know our neighbors.

As I watched Frank's black hands exploring Connie's body, I wondered if the Millers next door had noticed a black man arriving. George and Sue Miller were not really friends, just people we waved at when we saw each other in the yard. What if they did see, I asked myself? Even though Connie and I had accepted The Lifestyle and felt comfortable participating in Lifestyle activities, there was no way to shake all the guilt that came along with it. Not guilt for something we thought was wrong, guilt for being different; guilt because other people had decided that these were *bad things* that we did. Fuck the Millers, I thought.

It was becoming obvious to me that Frank and Connie would be fucking soon, and just as I angled my head as if to say, "What's next?" I saw Connie whispering into his ear. I knew she was suggesting that they move the party back to the bedroom.

I saw Frank nodding and he eased back from her and they both began to rise up from the sofa, Frank helped Connie to her feet and I wondered if perhaps, she might be a bit dizzy. I know I was, but the source of my light-headedness had come from Jim Beam, not the lips of a black man.

I stayed where I was, taking another sip from my glass, as they turned towards the hallway that led to the bedroom. I wasn't really sure what I should do, stay where I was or follow. I wasn't really sure I knew what I wanted to do. However, Connie made the decision for me.

As the two of them reached the hallway, Frank's arm around her, Connie looked over her shoulder at me. She motioned with her head silently but my ears heard her saying, "What the fuck, why are you still sitting there? You got to see this, come on dammit!" I nodded that I would follow.

Friend, your original email message to me did not include anything about what you and your wife have experienced yet so I don't know if she has gone black or not yet. If she hasn't, regardless of what I tell you, you won't really know what it is like to see it about to happen until you experience it yourself.

Imagine if you will, the trepidation you experience during the early springtime when there remains a touch of coolness in the air. You're standing on the edge of a swimming pool. You have reached down with the tip of your big toe and you know that the water is cold. You also know you want to go for a swim. Do you walk over to the shallow end of the pool and step down the concrete steps one at a time to get used to the water or do you yell, "Yee-ha" and jump?

My main concern at that moment was that I did not see any concrete steps. Connie and Frank were already out of site now, and I had few doubts that both of them would be naked before they reached the bed, one dick, one pussy, once they are connected, that's fucking.

I took a deep breath, and rose up out of my chair. I reached down for my highball glass and saw that it was nearly empty. I walked over to the kitchen counter to refresh it, at least I thought I was walking, I was just slightly beyond tipsy.

I filled my glass with ice but then thought about how quickly a standard highball glass would be emptied. I reached into the pantry for an iced tea glass. I poured my ice into it, and then added some more to it before grabbing the bottle of Jim Beam and emptying it into the glass. I smiled when I realized that even with all that liquor in the glass, there was still enough room for a little coke to sweeten it up.

That's when I remembered that Connie and I had failed to have lunch and I was hungry. I thought to myself, we shoulda ate something first. Can't watch my wife fucking a black man on an empty stomach, what the fuck?

The only thing I could find in the refrigerator was an opened package of Nathan's hotdogs. That'll work, I thought. I grabbed two of them from the package, taking note that there were two more in case I wanted more later on. I held one of the wieners up and inspected its elongated shape. "Dick food," I laughed, "made from the finest pigs lips and assholes money can buy." I bit off a quarter of the dog and it tasted marvelous.

I've been a fan of Nathan's for many years. Even cold, those doggies taste great. I took another bite, this time chewing repeatedly as I enjoyed the texture and taste of it. Too quickly, that first dog was gone and I grabbed my tea glass and washed it down. Turning my attention to the second wiener, it too was half gone before I knew it and I took another large sip of my drink. That second hotdog would already be in my stomach by the time I reached our bedroom, however before heading back, I opened the fridge back up and grabbed the remaining two.

As expected, Frank was balls deep inside Connie by the time I finally arrived. I doubt they noticed when I came in. Connie's legs were high in the air, supported by Frank's shoulders. I heard her moaning with pleasure before I even entered the room.

We had decorated our bedroom a bit like a motel room in that besides the standard mirrored and tallboy dressers, we had a small table and two chairs. I set my half-empty glass on the table and took a seat. However, as soon as I sat down, I realized that I needed to pee so I got back up, brushing against the table, nearly knocking my buddy Jim Beam over. Careful there fella, I thought.

I wasn't really watching what was happening on the bed at that moment, I was more focused on reaching the toilet without any further accidents. I could hear Connie as she apparently reached her first climax as I watch the mostly clear urine flow into the bowl. I had to pinch it off for a moment because I hadn't lifted the seat up. Good thing Connie didn't see that.

Relieved, I made my way back over to my chair and sat down, grabbing my glass first to make sure it wouldn't get knocked over. It was watching time now, and I sat back to enjoy the show. Frank and Connie were definitely putting on a performance, but not necessarily for me. They had changed position now, to the more traditional missionary form.

I sat there, fascinated by the visuals going on eight feet away from me. Occasionally, I took another sip although I noticed that the ice had watered down the alcohol and coke mixture. I knew there was no more liquor in the house and I was far too tipsy to drive over to the liquor store for more so I made do.

If there was a major feeling I had, other than a little queasy, it was a feeling of being detached. I was a part of what was going on in that room but only by the leanest definition. I wondered how long they would fuck. It seemed to me that already, it was probably twice as long as I had ever seen Connie do before and Frank showed no signs of finishing nor did it appear that Connie was through either.

Just then, the two began to switch positions again into a doggy style with Frank standing up near the edge of the bed. It was the first time I saw his cock. It was the biggest fucking appendage I had ever seen in my life and, he wasn't wearing a condom. I remembered Connie's words from the night Denise came to play, "I don't like them either. It feels so much better when the man fills you up. It really makes you feel like a woman."

She's one hundred percent woman tonight, I thought. If the amount of cum that was likely to pour out of Frank's dick was in line with the size of his massive big black cock, Connie's vessel would be overflowing for sure, maybe running down the side of the bed, perhaps even down the hallway and into the living room. I'll need to watch where I step, I thought.

It was eight o'clock when I woke up, or came to actually. It was dark in the room and dark outside as well. I had no idea what time it was until I looked at my watch.

I was alone in the bedroom, and I immediately wondered where Connie was. As I stood up, I realized that I was still a little drunk so using the walls to steady myself, I wondered down the hallway. Connie was setting in my easy chair watching television. There was no sign of Frank.

"Good morning," she said, as she saw me stagger into the room. "You want your chair?"

"Yes," I said, I wasn't yet capable of anything more coherent, but added, "it's not morning."

"Oh," Connie chuckled, "I know that, just didn't know if you knew."

I managed a smile at that; obviously, Connie was in a playful mood after her experience. That told me she had enjoyed her romp with Frank. "So, how did you like Frank?"

"He was fun," she allowed, and I noticed her trying to restrain a smile. "What did you think of him?"

"I didn't really get to know him," I told her, "I think he is fine if you enjoyed yourself. But, I guess my real question is about this interracial thing."

Connie looked somewhat distant as she tried to formulate a response. I was about to say something else to her when she finally began to speak.

"When I first saw his email and that he was black, well I guess I was sort of in shock. It just wasn't anything I'd ever really given any thought to before. When I replied, telling him I wanted to stay with my own race. Well afterwards, I just thought that was the wrong thing to say. It made me feel like a racist."

"I never thought you were a racist, and I didn't think you telling him that made you one either, I mean, well maybe it did if you think about it but if some man emails you who is in his sixties, saying you prefer to stay within your own age group doesn't mean you are racist against older guys. It just means you have a preference, a comfort zone."

"I suppose, maybe it is just the whole politically correct thing, choosing to not get with your grandpa is an accepted practice, you're excluding him because of his age and you know what, they call that age discrimination but, when you're talking about people having sex, age discrimination is legal, acceptable, even morally approved by the majority." Connie stated.

This was all a bit too heavy and deep for me at that moment, but I tried to stay with her despite my headache. "It doesn't matter what people call it, it boils down to your own personal preferences and when you are talking about sex, using your body, well, I guess if there is one place left where you can hang up a sign that reads, "Management reserves the right to refuse service to anyone," then this would be it.

"Of course," she replied, "but regardless, I shouldn't have written him that I stayed with my own race. I should have just said not interested, or anything except saying no because he was black."

"I understand," I said, "but still, it's you body we're talking about, not his right to vote or to be served in the diner or anything. I mean, no one has the… God given *right* to use *your body*."

"I know, I know, but anyway, that's what I was thinking after I sent him that reply. I just felt I'd screwed up and I wanted to make it right."

"So, you let him fuck you because you're white and he's black?" I said.

"No," she slammed back, "not at all. I just decided that I should give him the same chance, the same opportunity that I would have given a white guy. So, that's why I sent him another message."

"Okay, okay, I understand what you're saying."

"When I sent him that email, I was simply agreeing to meet him. You know me, I never promise someone I'll have sex with them, not if I don't know them already, or been with them before."

I knew better than to comment back to her that it was a pretty rare situation when she met someone in the lifestyle where she didn't end up fucking him. I tried to remember what I was thinking between the time she talked to him on the phone and the minute he walked in the door. Did I assume there would be sex? I admitted to myself that if it had been a white guy, that yes I would have assumed it would lead to playtime. I wasn't able to predict on this one.

"It sure didn't take long after he walked in before you two were going at it," I said, rather than stating, "That's the fastest anyone has ever gotten into your pants."

"When I agreed that he could come over, honestly I was just trying to make amends, give him a chance to meet us. I really didn't think anything would happen."

I asked, "So what changed your mind?"

Connie paused again, as she tried to work out the details and rationalizations in her own mind before speaking. What was very evident to me was that for us both, this had been a milestone event.

As I waited for her to speak, I quickly reviewed as many of Connie's partners as I could remember and I thought about Joey. Joey was far from Connie's type yet she had been with him many times before he had moved away. He had even achieved a relationship with her that was more than just fuck buddies. She had been with older guys, younger guys, Italians even; I chuckled quietly.

"When he first walked in, nothing had changed in my mind. I was still assuming that this would just be a meeting. We'd chat for a while and then when we ran out of things to say, one of us would say something like, "Thanks for stopping by, it was nice to meet you," and that would be the end of it.

"So, what happened?"

"I don't really know," she said, "but, you remember, he came over and sat down next to me and immediately, he laid his hand on my leg."

"Yeah, I remember that."

"That's when I knew."

"That's when you knew?"

"At first, when he first put his hand on me, I started to pull away from him but, I didn't and I don't know why I didn't. And, well, I don't know or understand what happened. You got up to fix yourself a drink and he pulled me over to him and I let him kiss me and, well I just…"

"I understand," I said, although I wasn't sure I really did other than to bring up the whole big head, little head thing where logic doesn't matter. "So, okay, you just went along with it and let it happen. So now what? You did it, how was it?"

"Well, once I got past that first touch, and I kissed with him and we embraced, it just turned into such an erotic and exciting thing. His being black seemed to make it so much better. Without a doubt, it was the best time I'd ever had with anyone."

"Really," I observed.

"It's hard for me to explain because I don't really understand."

"Are you going to do him again?" I asked.

"Oh hell yes," she replied quickly, "if he wants to."

Connie and I continued to talk that evening, and one of the things she told me was that he made her feel as if her pleasure was more important than his own. I asked her about his size and she told me that at first, it was really painful. She said, "I guess I'm bigger down there than I thought I was."

We never saw Frank again after that one afternoon. I guess he was just marking off notches on his belt. I remember Connie going on line quite a few times over the two or three days that followed and I guess from my perspective, she moved pretty quickly when the phone rang, but he never called back.

One thing I knew was, that it had also been quite an experience for me, I just wish I hadn't been drinking and passed out. Maybe that's why I kept bringing up the subject of her doing another black man.

Initially, she seemed uninterested in trying to connect with another black man but I finally suggested that maybe we could just add a line to our profile *about race not an issue* and she said, "Yeah, that's fine."

I think I thought at the time that once I saved the changes to our profile, that we'd have another black man contacting us immediately but that didn't happen. That really surprised me too because I had worked up my own fantasies about it, that there would be dozens of black men wanting to fuck a white woman.

I honestly don't know why I became so driven about the interracial thing, all I knew was that I wanted to have another chance to watch her and this time, at the most I planned to limit myself to maybe just one *social* drink. I think I irritated Connie a little because I started making suggestions to her that maybe we should send out our own invite to a couple of likely candidates. However, that isn't Connie's style. Not sure what it is exactly, but she prefers that people contact us first.

Finally, about two weeks after Frank and come over, we got an email message on *SwingPartners*. It was from a black couple that lived over ninety miles away. Normally, I wouldn't have given them any thought because of the distance. I also wasn't sure how I felt about going black myself.

Their message asked whether we ever visited their area also, which told me that most likely, we would need to travel to them. Their hometown was the opposite direction from what traveling we did do to occasionally visit with Connie's parents and her sister Beth.

I showed the message to Connie and she had her concerns as well on the distance plus the man didn't attract her and she said as much about that. I think that the only real notice I paid to the woman was the color of her skin.

"That's nearly two hours one way, four hours on the road just to meet someone," I said. "That's more time then I'd like to spend in a single day."

"I know, but maybe we could just get a motel room for the night, something cheap just so we don't have to drive back that day," Connie pointed out.

That pretty much told me that she was interested enough to consider it; in fact, it told me she was very interested in it. I wondered also if her primary desire also was the fact that they were black.

I said, "It doesn't cost anything to send them an email." Connie nodded and I began to type out a message to them.

"Thanks for contacting us; no unfortunately, we don't get out your way very often however we're not ruling it out."

I went on to give them some basic background information such as how long we had been in the lifestyle and I made a point of mentioning that Connie had just recently enjoyed her first interracial experience. I did not mention that I had never been with a black girl.

Their message had been sent to us the previous evening, a Sunday and our response went out the following Monday evening. Tuesday morning, over coffee before I started my morning prepping for work routine, I logged in and there was a new message from the couple, it was written by the female, Chantil.

As ours had been, their message included some general background information including the fact that they were somewhat new to the lifestyle. What I thought was the most interesting comment was that the husband Dennis had never been with a white woman and that was his big fantasy. She didn't reveal whether she had been with a white man before. I wrote back that if they were interested, that we would also like to meet them. That evening, I saw their reply and they asked us if we'd like to stop by their home Saturday evening, and then the four of us would go out to dinner.

I called Connie over and showed her their message and she remarked, "Sounds like fun. We could go earlier in the day, get a motel room and see the local sights, then meet them for dinner and see where that goes."

I sent them another message indicating that we would like to meet them for dinner Saturday night. We got a response from them about fifteen minutes later, which included their address and a suggestion to arrive at around seven Saturday evening.

"I wish they had included a phone number," I said, "Do you think we should send them ours? Perhaps suggest that they should call us so we can't get to know each other a little first?"

"No, it's fine. Just send them a message telling them we will see them Saturday at seven."

I typed in a brief acceptance message, sent it and then copied and pasted their address into MapQuest. I told Connie, "I'm going to find a hotel room close to where they live. That way, we have a place to stay and we don't know if they can even play at their house, they might have children at home."

"Sounds like a plan," Connie smiled.

There was a Red Roof Inn about two miles from where Chantil and Dennis lived and I booked us in, requesting early check-in. Connie asked me if I was excited about being with a black woman and I told her that frankly, I wasn't turned on by the idea but I was curious.

She laughed and said, "Once you go black..."

I laughed and said, "Well, is that your story?"

"Maybe," she smiled. I didn't know if she was joking or not and I didn't know if I wanted to know.

Of course, Connie and I spent a lot of time talking about our upcoming meeting with Chantil and Dennis, plus we talked about some site seeing ideas while we were in their town. We often discussed planned future meetings but this one; we felt we knew the least about so there was a lot of speculation about it. One key element we talked about was the use of private signals between us such as did she like him and did I like her or should one of us make a move, etc. Unfortunately, this grew into such a complicated mess that we both finally just agreed to go and see where things led. Alas, Dennis was not destined to be Connie's second interracial encounter.

Connie had a dentist appointment that Thursday afternoon and it was so late in the day that she just came home after her semi-annual teeth scrapping session. She had logged into *SwingPartners* to see if we had any mail. I suspect she was mostly wanted to insure that Chantil and Dennis hadn't canceled on us.

When I arrived home, as soon as I walked in the door she announced that she had a date. "Who with?" I asked.

"He's a new guy, his name is Norton."

"Norton? Is that his first name or his last name?" I asked.

"I don't know he just said he was Norton."

As I was trying to get my head around the man's name, she added, "He's black!"

"Oh?" I said, "And you have a 'date' date?"

"Yes, he's taking me to dinner."

"I see," I said, as I sat down in my easy chair. I was a little put off by the fact that this was a date, meaning that whatever happened might happen elsewhere. Even her basic getting to know you, which had been damn little with Frank, had been where I could observe. "What's he look like?"

"I don't know, I logged in, there was an email and his profile wasn't filled out."

"Show me," I said.

Connie sat down and logged in as I looked over her shoulder. She clicked on the latest email, which was from someone called **JazzLover**. The email was pretty minimal.

"I read your profile and I'd like to take you out to dinner. Please call me at 555-9712. Norton"

"Show me his profile." I said.

"Okay," she said, amused because she already knew what I was going to see. His profile was completely empty, with the words *Prefer Not to Say* on everything except his ID and location. "At least he's local," I said. "So, how did you end up with a date?"

"Well, I just decided to call him and see who he was, what he was like. He had a nice voice, pleasant manor, in fact I had already made up my mind that I'd like to meet him sometime before I found out he was black."

"Once you go black," I joked.

"Maybe," she smiled, "Maybe you'll find out yourself this weekend."

"Maybe," I replied.

"Okay, well I need to get cleaned up for my date. Can you take care of yourself the rest of the evening? There are plenty of leftovers in the frig."

I gave her a slight snarl, as I made the mental comparison between steak house food and two-day-old meat loaf. I asked, "Where is he taking you, McDonalds?"

"Maybe," she said, as she headed back towards the bedroom to get ready.

When Connie had a date, it was a mixed bag for me. I enjoyed creating mental images as I pictured the event in my mind. It always seemed to play out as a collection of scenes, and not necessarily in order although I usually managed to use the clock to establish when a given scene might be going on.

Connie was always after me to make contact with some single ladies occasionally and have dates of my own but so far, I hadn't, mainly because I consider myself rather traditional and if I took a date out to eat or to the movies, I expected to pay for things. I also expected Connie's date to cover her expenses but occasionally, she spent some of our money to pay for things when she wanted to do something nice for her escort. I didn't like that, as it was an unexpected expense and our budget was like most peoples, tight.

However, I will be the first to admit that I wouldn't mind having a lady friend over, to sit around snuggled up under a blanket watching movies on TV while Connie was out. But, to be honest, I would be just as happy to have one of my guy friends over for a few beers or to watch something on ESPN.

However, all my drinking buddies would have shit themselves if they knew Connie was out running around with some other guy.

I looked at the meatloaf in the refrigerator and opted to make a burger run later that evening when I started getting hungry. I decided to busy myself with a little television and channel surfing.

Norton arrived exactly on schedule at seven; Connie was still getting dressed when he arrived. I was surprised at his appearance. He was good looking, shaved head, and he obviously worked out. From his build, I'd wager that he worked out a lot. One look and I had no doubt that Connie was fucked!

I invited him in and he turned out to be a very polite and consider individual. I took an instant liking to him. He also appeared to be at perfect ease being around me. I offered him a drink but he turned me down, stating he doesn't drink and drive except perhaps one glass of wine over dinner, another point for him in my book.

I asked him where they were going, which part of me said wasn't my business but he was very open about his plans. He told me that he was going to suggest one of the local Italian Bistros and wanted to know if Connie might prefer somewhere else. In fact, he asked a lot of questions about what Connie's likes and dislikes were. I realized that I was giving him a huge advantage over my wife but I felt that the more he knew, the better her experience would be.

I kept wondering what was taking Connie so long, as Norton and I chatted. I didn't ever bother to ask him if Norton was his first or last name, it just didn't seem to be an important matter. Norton was what he preferred, so Norton it would be.

His questions about her favorite restaurants began to get more personal. He asked if she liked massage, kissing, her favorite position and I pretty much laid things out for him. Just before Connie finally made an entrance, Norton leaned over and asked if it would be all right with me if he took her back to his apartment after dinner, and if he could bring her home in the morning.

The next day would be Friday and I knew she wouldn't want to call in sick so I told him that she probably wouldn't want to make a late night of it. He seemed to take it in stride saying, "That's cool, I understand. I have to be up early too."

Regardless of whether Connie would return before morning, I knew that if they ended up screwing, it would be at his place, and one look at Norton and I knew they would end up screwing. With her still in the bedroom, hopefully putting on her final makeup touches, I wanted so much to go back and have some fun with her, saying, "I know a secret…"

I heard Connie announce, "Hello," from over my shoulder as she came into the living room. I could almost hear how pleased she was at what Norton looked like in her voice with that one word.

Norton arose and walked over to greet her. I turned around on my seat just in time to see him take her into an embrace and kiss her. I think she was a bit taken off guard by this but no doubt, she kissed him back.

After Connie asked me for the third time if I was going to be all right until she got home, they finally left. My only objection was that I had already seen all there would be for me to see. Connie's farewell remark as she headed out the door was, "We shouldn't be out too late," and I just nodded.

About an hour after Connie left on her date, I ended up calling for a pizza delivery, and around ten o'clock I called it a night. Just in case, I settled in to the spare bedroom. My bladder was cruel to me that night and at just before three in the morning, I woke up to pee. I glanced in our bedroom and the bed was still made. Even thought I knew Norton wanted her for the night, and despite how much I assumed Connie would be attracted to him, I was a bit surprised she hadn't come home.

When the alarm went off at seven thirty, it was relatively easy for me to hop out of bed. This time, I wasn't surprised to see that Connie still hadn't returned. Thirty-five minutes later, I was out the door on my way to work. I tried calling her around ten AM but her cell phone must have been turned off. By lunchtime, I was starting to get worried.

I couple of my co-workers asked me to go to lunch with them, and I tried to beg off but ended up going anyway. They didn't seem to notice how preoccupied I was. The night before, my mind had done its job and provided visuals about what might be going on, however, my limited experience in seeing Connie being black-fucked wasn't very clear.

Upon my return from lunch, I had a voice mail on my office phone from Connie. All she said was, "I'm fine, sorry I didn't call earlier; can you pick me up at work on your way home?" I tried calling her back at work but got her voice mail and her cell phone was still turned off. I assumed she must have left it on the bedroom dresser.

At least I knew she wasn't lying in a ditch somewhere, beaten and raped, and worse. That is one of the problems of living on the edge, meeting strangers just because they put up an online profile. Many of the people we know are only known to us by first name, we don't even know where some of our friends live. But, Connie was fine apparently, so I was able to mostly focus on getting my job done for the remainder of the afternoon.

Connie was standing outside her building when I pulled up just after five that day. As she sat down next to me she joked, "Dropped off at work by one man, picked up by another. I wonder if anyone noticed?"

"So, how was it?"

"Oh I had a great time. Norton is really nice and I liked the way he treated me."

"So, how was he?"

"Great."

I waited on her to elaborate but after six more blocks, I realized she was more intent on staring out the car window than talking. "Well, fill me in, tell me what happened?"

"Relax Baby, I'll tell you everything but I am so tired. Can we stop and grab some take out? I really just want to eat and go to bed. We'll have a lot of time to talk on our way to see Dennis and Chantil tomorrow."

I was insanely interested to hear the details but I knew Connie couldn't be pushed. If I did, she'd just get pissed and clam up on me completely. After the years she and I have been together, I knew which buttons to push and which ones to stay away from. I knew I could get something out of her, but nothing too in depth. If I only had one or two questions to ask, I needed to be sure and pick the most important ones.

"How about tacos?" I asked.

"Sure," she said.

As I pulled into the fast food drive through, I thought about what I knew. Of course, the primary question of did she fuck him, I knew that would happen before she even saw him herself the night before. He had a good personality, looked great, and I knew he wanted to do her even before he saw her, not to mention that she had spent the night at his apartment.

I think the question I most wanted answered was the one that I'd had ever since that day Frank came to the house. I never saw Connie giving him head although I assumed she had, but I was probably already passed out by then.

"Did you suck his big black cock?" was the question I wanted to ask but that just sounded so hardcore that I couldn't bring myself to ask it. Besides, I assumed she probably had anyway. But, I wondered, did she swallow? I wondered if Norton wore

60

a condom or did he fill Connie's vessel with essence of Norton?

By the time I had surrendered my debit card to the cashier at the Mexican place, I had settled on one question to ask her. As we pulled back onto the road I said, "Hearing about your exciting evening on the road tomorrow is fine Honey, let me just ask you one question."

"Sure," she said, "I think I can handle that, you want to know if we fucked?"

"Nope," I said smugly, "I know you fucked, what I want to know is whether you are going to see him again."

Connie looked at me; I think she was a little perturbed that I already knew what she thought I was going to ask. "Yes, I plan on seeing him again, maybe often. He asked me out for tomorrow night but I told him you and I already had plans. He asked about next Friday night and I said yes. Also, while we're on the subject. Don't make any weekend plans for next weekend. I may end up spending it with Norton."

I was a little surprised by her answer, and not sure I cared for it that much either. I didn't have a problem with her going out on dates and spending the night out occasionally, even a weekend once in a while was all right but the way she was talking about this Norton fellow, I was beginning to feel a bit squeezed and she only met the guy less than twenty-four hours earlier.

As She had indicated, Connie consumed her share of tacos and told me she was going to take her bath and then go to bed. She advised me to get to bed early too because we had that long drive the next day. I promised her I wouldn't stay up late but frankly, I was hoping I could even get to sleep.

I had this Norton person on my mind plus who could possibly guess what might happen the next evening with Dennis and Chantil. I finally fell asleep sometime after midnight despite climbing in bed with Connie just after ten. She was already asleep even then, exhausted I suppose.

Okay, friend, sorry to be so long winded on this but you said you wanted the whole story. It really doesn't come out right unless you understand the steps that led to Connie's boyfriend. Norton was just another one of those steps although she did see him numerous times after that first date.

The next morning was nearly over before we finally managed to get the bags packed and into the car. Despite my lack of sleep the night before, I felt refreshed and full of anticipation. I realized that a big part of our trip to meet Dennis and Chantil was the trip itself.

I think I may have waited until we were at least two miles down the highway before I started asking about Connie's date with Norton. It wasn't that she acted as if there was some big secret, and every question I asked was answered but to me, it seemed as though her answers were as limited as she could make them. I don't think she was doing it on purpose however; I couldn't help but wonder if she was starting to consider her solo activities to be somehow, her business and not mine.

This probably unintended reluctance to provide details is a key factor why I am so happy with where we are today, but I'm getting way ahead of my story. Let's see, where was I...

We got into town and it didn't take us long to find the Red Roof Inn where I had made a reservation. We checked in, hauled in all our bags, one small gym bag for me, two large suitcases for Connie, plus one really large book bag which held my toothbrush and my brand of tooth paste and a razor. The rest was lipsticks, powders, perfumes, various tools of which mostly, I was clueless about their function. I grabbed my swimsuit and headed to the pool while Connie organized the drawers. She said she'd join me in a few minutes. She did an hour later.

"Come on and get in, the water is great!" I yelled to her.

"No, I don't want to get my hair wet," she said, and she found a sunny spot and climbed onto one of those poolside chaise lounges. I just shook my head because I guarantee you that her hair dryer was in the motel room. I assumed her iron and that small travel ironing board was there as well. I'm convinced to this day that if we ever made plans for an extended vacation, like two weeks somewhere, I'd need to get our house raised up so we could put wheels on it and haul it with us just to carry the essentials.

As Connie soaked up rays, I frolicked around in the pool like a teenager and I started thinking about the evening to come. I started to wonder about what Connie had said about once I went black. Would I or would I not? Connie's last two partners had been black and I assumed that number three would be also before the night was over. In addition, unless something unexpected came along mid-week, Connie would be fucking and sucking big black cock again with Norton.

Although we had planned on checking out some local sights, the pool took most of the afternoon and what was left of it was spent napping in our motel room. I was fine with that, the pool was fun and I knew it could be a late night. That is one aspect of this lifestyle that over time might become a problem. We both had identical schedules of Monday through Friday, eight to five, with weekends off. Before we started staying up late fucking people, we usually went to bed every night including weekends around ten or so and got up early just as if it was a workday. It seems like anytime we do make party plans on a weekend, Monday morning is there and you wonder where all that time went that you felt was yours when you left the office on Friday.

I was the first to awake and I realized we were going to be late if we didn't hurry up and get dressed and on the road over to meet Dennis and Chantil. "Why did you let me sleep so late," Connie screamed, as she ran into the bathroom. Miraculously, an hour later we were knocking on their door.

Dennis and I shook hands and he gave Connie a welcome embrace. Once inside, I caught my first view of Chantil. She looked quite a bit better than her picture, and she was dressed in a short, tight red dress that accented her curves quite well. Did I mention that it was slit up the side nearly to her waist?

I remember thinking at the time that although I really liked the way she was dressed, I was glad we weren't in our own home town where we might get spotted by some of our straight friends, not that we had that many anymore. As I said, she looked great but you can go overboard with this stuff.

Occasionally, Connie wore similar outfits but only when we went to swinger parties and we didn't get out of the car going or coming to the party. Connie even got into the car while I still had it in the garage at home.

Of course, if the neighbors happened to look out and see her in too sexy an outfit that was probably nothing compared to the eyebrow raises she might have generated when she left the house the previous Thursday with Norton.

After filling Dennis and Chantil in on all the details about our drive there and an afternoon at the pool; Dennis said, "Let's go, I'm starved," and we all agreed that it was time for dinner.

I was expecting that the conversation would center around the lifestyle, as Dennis and I rode in the front seat of his car with Chantil and Connie in the back seat but that wasn't the case. Despite Chantil's fuck me outfit, the conversation was very generic and across a number of topics ranging from politics to religion, films we had seen, places we had visited.

Nothing changed as we waited the forty-five minutes for our table to be ready and once it was our turn to be seated, I was surprised that Dennis and Chantil slid into the same side of the booth together. Every time Connie and I had gone out to eat with other swinger couples, I always sat with the other man's wife and vice versa. Even when Connie and I went out with one of her single guy friends, she would sit on his side and usually, there was a little action going on under the table out of sight from at least most of the other people in the restaurant.

By the time we finished our meal, I was convinced that this was only going to be a meet, and fully expected either Dennis or Chantil to start yawning as we pulled back into their driveway, followed by one of them commenting that it had been a long day and Church started early the next morning. My biggest fear was what Connie would say, because she had turned down a date with Norton to come with me.

We had just turned into their street, which I recognized by noting the McDonalds that was located on the left before we made the turn, sure enough, I heard a yawn coming from the back seat. It didn't sound like it came from Connie. A few minutes later, I heard Chantil exclaim, "Excuse me."

As we piled out of the car, I just stood waiting, expecting to hear how it had been such a pleasant evening. It actually had been nice, but I wish I hadn't needed to drive nearly a hundred miles plus get a motel room for it. I glanced at Connie and I could see that she was thinking the same thing I was. In fact, she was easing her way towards the passenger side door on our car.

"You folks ready to get down and play?" Dennis said.

I was shocked. It just hadn't seemed that this was where things had been destined to go. For a moment, the thought occurred to me that once inside, Dennis would go to the closet and pull out a Monopoly game or a deck of cards.

"Sure," I said, "Connie?"

"Ah, sure," she said, obviously as surprised as I was.

"Fine," said Dennis, "Let's go inside. Robert, you a drinkin' man?"

"Yeah, socially now and then," I said, as I remembered how drunk I had gotten when Connie had fucked Frank.

Once inside, Dennis showed us his available stock. I had mixed feelings when I saw one of the bottles labeled Jim Beam. "Bourbon, and coke if you have it."

"Connie?"

"Rum and coke," she said.

Dennis handed me his drink but I had watched him as he poured in the Jim Beam. It was at least a double, and I swore to myself that this would be my one and only drink that night.

I've often wondered if perhaps, I might be an alcoholic. I really don't drink that often but I tend to overdo it when I do. I can't seem to stop at just one to be social. However, I vowed that if I had another drink that night, it would be water on the rocks or just plain coke.

Connie's drink was too strong for her as well and she only sipped at it, waiting on the ice to water it down some. The four of us were all sitting in the living room and I wondered how things would progress from there on. I didn't feel comfortable moving over and sitting next to Chantil. Other than Dennis' somewhat cryptic remark, the subject of sex remained unmentioned.

Another hour passed, and I felt the urge for another drink but managed to refuse Dennis' offer for a refill. We were still talking about everything and every subject under the sun except fucking. I was about to stage my own yawn, and talk about the long drive we had ahead of us the next morning.

67

Okay friend; let me summarize things just a little bit for you before I go on. This whole thing, Connie being with a black man and seeing her do it had managed to become a gigantic frustration for me.

True, I had seen Frank pounding her the week before but it had been shrouded in a fog for me. All I could muster were some brief and singular images of that day. With Norton, all I had was a few very reserved comments from Connie that offered no glimpses whatsoever. Just then, I yawned.

The yawn wasn't staged, I was actually getting sleepy and highly alcoholic drink wasn't helping. I was about to mention that long drive when Dennis started talking.

"We really only have one rule," he said, "I hope it isn't a problem for you. Chantil and I, well we like to play in separate rooms, with the doors closed. You folks okay with that?"

Of course, I thought, of course Connie is going to get black fucked tonight and of course, I won't be there to see it. How bloody likely is this scenario?

I really was at a loss as to what to say. It wasn't that I really objected to playing in separate rooms, in fact, it was something I had yet to experience, at least as far as me being in a room behind a closed door. It didn't take me long to realize that had Dennis and Chantil just been another white swinger couple we had met on *SwingPartners*, that all of us having private solos would have seemed like a cool, novel idea.

Connie made the decision for us, by telling Dennis that we were fine with their preference. Regardless, it was still such a bazaar night; neither Connie nor I had physically touched either Dennis or Chantil yet apparently, we had all just agreed to swap wives and fuck.

"The bedrooms are this way," Dennis said, pointed towards the hallway. He immediately began walking in that direction. Connie rose up from her seat and followed him, perhaps six feet behind. Chantil also got up and she was perhaps another six feet behind Connie. I pulled up the rear, maintaining that same six-foot spacing. I couldn't help but think how cold blooded this felt. As I felt I was expected to do, I closed the door to the bedroom Chantil had selected. I assumed it was one of the secondary bedrooms. She walked over to the nightstand and switched on the lamp. She opened the nightstand drawer, pulled out a large silk scarf, and covered the lamp with it, changing the rooms lighting noticeably. She asked me to switch off the overhead light. I realized that Dennis and Chantil had their routine down pat. I wondered if the other bedroom also had a color scarf for atmosphere.

Chantil wasted little time in removing that sexy outfit of hers, and taking my cue from her, I also began to shed clothes as rapidly as possible but she was already lying on the bed by the time my last sock hit the corner of the room where I'd tossed everything else.

"All right then," I said, my dick still growing but nearly ready to be used. At that moment, what Connie might be doing wasn't high on my priority list. At that moment, my first taste of chocolate was wrapped in my arms and chocolate lips touched mine.

Everything was familiar of course, there was no doubt I was touching a woman's body yet there were slight differences.

Obviously, the imagery of her dark skin was completely new for me but the smells, the touch, alien but not unpleasantly so, not by any means. In fact, almost from the beginning when my hand covered her luscious and soft breast, I started to gain an understanding of what Connie had discovered. Maybe I won't be going back to white either.

Although Chantil had been very quiet and reserved all night long, once we were together in bed naked, she turned into a wild cat, pulling at me, scratching at my back, wrapping her legs around my body that even if I wanted to, I could not extricate myself from her grip.

Inside, inside her pussy, again it was familiar yet somehow wildly different. I had to investigate this further. I whispered, "Let me go down on you, Baby."

Chantil loosened her leg lock on me and allowed me to slide down her body, and I kissed and licked every inch of her all the way down. Did I taste chocolate? No, but whatever it was that dazzled my tongue tasted wonderful. When my lips first touched her clit, I thought she was going to scream from pleasure. Her whole body tightened and began to shake as I licked and probed everything I found.

It occurred to me that either Chantil rarely received oral or she loved it more than life herself. Either way, I determined myself to give her the best tongue-lashing I could for as long as she wanted, and she wanted it for a long time that night. When finally I felt the need to shove my cock back into her cunt, she rewarded me with pelvic movements befitting a contortionist.

I got so deep into her that it felt as if my balls had partially pushed inside her. I moved my hand down to her clit and added additional stimulation. As a reward, she sucked on my tongue until I thought she might pull it out by its root but I didn't mind that at all.

So, this is interracial sex huh? No wonder people enjoy it. I actually began to consider the idea of committing my life to fucking beautiful ebony ladies. Connie better watch out or I might trade her in for another color. Just kidding of course friend, but I was really digging being with Chantil.

The first time I came, I started to pull out but she wasn't finished with me, not yet by a long measure. She continued to slam into me, her long arms allowed her hands to grasp my buttocks and she used them to push and pull me into her. Finally, my cock spent, she wasn't able to retain it any longer and it slid out of her. Nevertheless, Chantil was still not ready for this round to end. She pushed down on my shoulders and I knew what she wanted.

Going down on a woman's vagina that was full of my own seed was something I had never done before. I had wanted to and many times with Connie, I had committed myself to the task however my release always seemed to dissipate my desires to the point where there simply wasn't an urge any longer. But, with Chantil, none of that mattered and I eagerly devoured everything my mouth and tongue could find below her waist.

When finally, that first round ended for us both, Chantil hopped off the bed and opened the bedroom door and left me alone. However, she returned a few moments later with a warm washcloth and gently cleaned up my cock and balls.

Afterwards, we clung to each other, our arms and legs entwined. It was possibly at that moment, having been in the dim lighting so long, my eyes were fully adjusted and I marveled at the contrasting colors between our bodies. Yes, I was hooked on black pussy.

I'm don't know how long we lay together, I know I was exhausted and Chantil seemed perfectly content to lie beside me and I slowly passed into a light sleep. I say light because I think I never lost consciousness for more than five or ten minutes at a time.

I'm not sure what time of night it was when I awoke from my latest catnap to the feel of a warm mouth wrapped around my cock. I wasn't long before it also started waking up. It felt so good that I almost felt as if I was floating, weightless about the room. Chantil was giving me the best blowjob I had ever experienced.

I wondered if I should interrupt her before I shot my load? I thought I had my answer when she briefly stopped sucking on me but then I realized that she wanted to mutually pleasure both of us orally at the same time. Even after I came, I continued to gnaw at her, biting, chewing, and probing with my tongue, all the while Chantil continued on me by kissing, licking, and sucking on my balls.

All of a sudden, I had an urge to do something I had never done before. I tried to pull her bottom down to me but my neck and tongue wouldn't extend far enough, not with her weight on me anyway. Finally, I gently pushed her over to my side and then rolled her over on her stomach. I spread her legs and gave my first rim job to her.

I'll admit, sticking my tongue inside of an asshole wasn't something I had spent hours fantasizing about, and although I felt compelled to perform this service at that moment, I didn't think it would become a regular tool in my arsenal, but who knows. All I know was that Chantil loved it and at that moment, I wanted to do anything for Chantil that she might enjoy. Before the night was over, I had sucked pussy, tits, asshole, and toes, and fingers. I'd bit into her lips and her neck, chewed on her labia, tongued her ears and I even tickled her underarms with my tongue.

Maybe I felt that my white cock might not compete with other cocks Chantil had experienced; maybe that was part of my driving force. Maybe it was just because I wanted to experience everything this black beauty could offer.

Finally, restful and extended sleep came for us both. When I awoke, I was alone. I think it was the smell of freshly brewed coffee that aroused me. I swiveled around and swung my legs around and slowly stretched them out until my feet hit the floor. I noticed that the brightly colored scarf on the nightstand lamp was gone. My body ached from the previous night's workout. I finally managed to stand up and slowly put my clothes on.

Dressed now, I opened the bedroom door. I noticed that the door to the bedroom where Connie had gone with Dennis was also open. It wasn't necessary for me to look to where the coffee was being served; my nose led me there.

I saw Connie, Dennis, and Chantil sitting around a dining room table. Connie noticed me and asked, "Coffee?"

"Coffee," I muttered, my mouth dryer than I realized. I was definitely dehydrated so I added, "and some water too."

Chantil headed to the pantry to grab a water glass while Connie poured my coffee, adding just the right amount of sugar to it. I couldn't help thinking how similar my taste in coffee and women were not, black and sweet.

After initially quenching my thirst with the water, I took my first sip from my coffee and I was amazed how quickly that one taste worked to clear out cobwebs in my head and clear my eyes.

I saw that like myself, everyone was fully dressed; although unlike Connie and I, Chantil and Dennis were dressed differently then they had been the night before. Chantil's outfit was more typical of someone you might encounter at the local supermarket rather than a working girl standing on a street corner. Frankly, I was already missing that dress she had worn the night before.

Satisfied that my initial needs had been satisfied, Chantil and Connie resumed their conversation with Dennis. They were talking about the benefits of organically grown food, which I found very boring.

I thought to myself, this is the Dennis and Chantil that we met last night when we first arrived. The same ones we went to dinner with also. It certainly wasn't the Chantil who spent the night with me; I wondered how different Dennis had been with Connie during their one on one encounter.

As they talked about carrots and tomatoes, I pondered on how people could departmentalize their life so much. Listening and looking at Chantil and Dennis that morning, there was no clue that they were swingers or that we four had swapped and fucked all night. The only thing I could not figure out was why Chantil dressed so erotically for dinner. It didn't seem to match everything else I had observed.

I noticed that a clock on the dining room wall indicated that it was just after eight in the morning. I had assumed that it would have been closer to noon. I knew I had not slept much the night before and seeing what time it was reminded me how spent my mind and body was.

"Would you folks care to join us at church this morning?" asked Dennis.

Connie and I had not attended church for several years, choosing to fall back on our own personal beliefs about what was right and what was wrong. However, the idea intrigued me somewhat as I envisioned an all black congregation, a large church choir, all the callouts and responses by the congregation and the musicians and robust preacher as I had seen in movies and on television and I was tempted to accept.

However, I also wondered if I would feel guilt as I stood next to a black woman in church whose butt had been explored thoroughly by my tongue only a few hours earlier. I'm not much for wanting to feel odd in public places so I responded with, "No, thanks for the offer but we need to get back home."

We left Chantil and Dennis' home a few minutes later and headed over to the motel to pick up our stuff, all of which lie neatly ordered in the dresser drawers and hanging from the clothes rack. I couldn't help notice the twin beds, neatly made just as they had been when we checked in the day before. I knew that next time we traveled to see new people; I'd wait on getting a motel room.

We grabbed fast food biscuits just before hitting the highway for home. Connie was strangely quiet and I asked her how her night had gone. She looked at me, smiled and said, "No complaints."

My mind asked questions, which I answered for it.

"Did you fuck?" *"Yes."*

"How many times?" *"Several, we fucked all night."*

"Did he have a big dick?" *"Yes, very big."*

"Did you suck his cock?" *"Of course, and I swallowed."*

I actually felt an urge to say something to Connie, about how it was getting on my nerves that she was so secretive and closed mouthed about her experiences with black men. She had not been that way before when she had gone out with white men. I ended up deciding that I should just let things be.

When we finally arrived home, neither of us wanted to do anything but go to bed and sleep. Connie woke me up around five that evening and cautioned me that if I slept any longer, I would wake up and then not be able to get back to sleep before it was time to go to work on Monday.

Two days later, we received that email from Jeremy that I mentioned at the beginning of the story. As you might well imagine by now, this wasn't the kind of email I hoped would arrive on the *SwingPartners* site. I wasn't at all excited about

Connie having yet another black on white experience where I was virtually excluded. However, I also felt that it wasn't my decision and I called Connie over to show her the email from Jeremy.

Connie looked at the email and commented that she thought it was very thoughtful and considerate, and of course she added that she would like to know more. I actually hadn't even clicked on his profile myself yet so as Connie sat beside me I brought it up.

His picture showed a man with a very friendly smile and just a hint that he might be a bit mischievous. He looked to be a little heavy but not bad. He didn't compare to Frank but then few men did. I was also impressed at how complete his profile was, and it was obvious that he had spent time on it and given his essay questions real meaning.

"You want to email him back?" I asked.

"Sure," said Connie.

I switched back to his initial email and clicked the reply link and began typing.

"Thank you for contacting us. This is Robert speaking, Connie is beside me."

"What else do you want me to say?" I asked.

"I don't know," said Connie, "should we just give him our phone number or should we tell him more about us?"

I'm not really sure what prompted me to say what I said next, I know it came out of my frustration. I told Connie, "You can tell in his letter that his primary interest is meeting you Honey, why don't you suggest that you two meet together out somewhere, like for a drink?"

"Oh, well, okay, I guess I could do that. Is that all right with you?"

No, it was not frankly, but sometimes you just have to push at something that doesn't fit right until you understand how it works. Rather than answer Connie directly, I just started typing again.

"Connie would like to meet you at in the bar at Garcia's Mexican Cuisine some evening this week around six o'clock. Let us know which night works best for you.

Robert and Connie"

I hit the send button before Connie could say anything. Two hours later, we received a response from Jeremy asking if meeting tomorrow night was possible. Before I even told Connie that we had another email, I typed our response.

"Yes, six o'clock Thursday evening at Garcia's Mexican Cuisine; look for a table with a black sequined cell phone case on it.

After sending it off, I told Connie about her date. This time, I was prepared for what would happen, making the assumption that Connie would leave for her rendezvous around 5:30 Thursday evening and that she would come home either late or not at all. At least with her driving her own car, I knew I wouldn't need to pick her up at work Friday.

Well friend perhaps that is one of the things about the lifestyle that makes it such a joy. Never ever anticipate, never assume, and life will be simpler. Expect the unexpected.

Thursday evening, Connie did rush home from work, quickly showered, and dressed for her date. She was less than ten minutes late getting out the door. I called out for pizza again, and discovered much to my delight that there were two cold bottles of beer in the refrigerator.

I had given up on trying to create fantasy images that would allow me to peek at what Connie was doing, at least with black men. It was funny however, for just a brief moment I caught a glimpse of an elderly couple setting in a booth just behind Connie. I think I was looking from her date's perspective.

In this fantasy, I overheard Connie declare, "It feels so much better when the man fills you up. It really makes you feel like a woman." Instantly, I saw the old woman's face as she placed her hand over her open mouth in shock and disgust. She could see that the man Connie was speaking to was black.

Unfortunately, that was all my imagination could produce for me that evening, and after watching an episode of *Law & Order* that must have been at least ten years old, I flipped off the TV and headed down the hallway to call it a night.

I started to go into the spare bedroom but thought, what's the point of that? Fifteen minutes later, I was fast asleep in my own bed. I wasn't asleep very long.

I think initially, I thought I was still dreaming, perhaps drifting along on a boat down a river but then I realized that I was being touched. Someone was gently stroking my back and immediately I recognized Connie's fingers.

I should mention a little additional background about Connie and me here. Connie is a massage whore. I don't mean that as being derogatory however. It's just that she loves massage so much that she'd give anything to get one. I might add that it always aroused me to give her a massage and one of my favorite things to do when I was wide-awake and needed to get to sleep was to start rubbing my hands over Connie's back and legs. Sure enough, not long after I started I would feel my dick coming online and my massaging also brought Connie to an aroused state and we'd end up having a quickie fuck and then we'd both finally be able to get to sleep.

Connie operated differently however. If she was wide awake and wanted to get to sleep, she would rub my back and for some reason, the repetitive motions she would use to massage me would cause her to slowly drift off to sleep. The funny thing is that when she did that, the gentle touch with only the slightest hint of fingernails on my back would also send me into a trancelike state that after a while would lead me to sleep as well.

Occasionally, if Connie finds herself awake, she will reach over and begin to massage my back even when I am asleep. Usually, this wakes me up but not always, and even when I do wake up, her gentle stroking up and down by shoulders usually floats me off again quickly.

As I awoke to her gentle touches that night, I immediately assumed that Connie must be somewhat hyperactive from her date and decided to use me to help her sleep. Admittedly, I was surprised that she was home at all. That's when I first realized that something else was going on. There was a movement of the bed itself happening.

If you imagine what it must feel like for people out in California when one of those minor earthquakes hits during the middle of the night, then you know how I felt. Instantly, I was awake and I rolled over to look to see if that was what was happening. I'd never experienced and earthquake before but I surmised that this must be what it feels like. Just then, I heard a deep and strange voice, which I instantly recognized as having African American roots.

"Hello Robert, nice to meet you."

The room was dark, but there was enough light to detect a dark shape on the other side of Connie.

"Huh?"

"I said, hello Robert, it's nice to meet you."

I realized now what was going on. Connie had brought her date home and they were fucking in my bed while I slept in it. I was not sure what to do about this unexpected situation.

"Ah, yeah… nice to meet you too," I mumbled. "You guys are… fucking?"

"Oh yes," cooed Connie.

"Oh, okay," I replied. I rolled back over on my side. I didn't really know what else to do at that precise moment. Connie and her friend seemed content to just continue fucking and Connie resumed her rhythmic rubbing on my back.

"Are you Jeremy?" I asked softly.

"Yes," Connie answered, "that's Jeremy."

I heard myself saying, "Nice to meet you Jeremy," but this was absolutely the strangest conversation I had ever had in my thirty plus years.

As I lie there on my side of the bed, I continued to feel the gentle rocking of the mattress below me and I also detected swishy sounds, which I knew must be coming from Connie's vagina. I wasn't sure if I was supposed to roll over and start participating or whether I should just lie there, as if nothing was going on. And, that was not going to be easy, ignoring that my wife was lying beside me getting fucked. I wondered what time it was.

I don't know what time they quit fucking because somehow, their gentle motions had rocked me back to sleep and I awoke the next morning. Of course, at first I was certain that I had dreamed everything and fully expected to turn over and find that I was alone in the bed, I wasn't.

Quietly, I got up and out of bed and grabbed my robe out of the closet. I had laid my wristwatch on the nightstand, I picked it up, and it read five minutes until seven. I knew Connie needed to get up and start getting dressed for work but I hated to disturb them.

That vision that morning of Connie in bed cuddled up with a black man was going to provide endless material for future fantasies, I was absolutely positive of that, plus I had the memories of being rocked to sleep in my own bed in that new and highly erotic style from the night before.

I wondered whose idea it had been to come back to our house to play. More so, I wondered what had made them decide to do climb in bed with me when there was another bedroom down the hall. I considered those all to be good questions that I'd ask when I had the chance.

"Connie," I said softly, but she didn't respond. I repeated her name a little louder but still no response. Finally, I walked back over to my side of the bed and leaned over and touched her arm; still nothing. One more time I tried to wake her, this time jostling her arm while calling out to her, "Connie, it's after seven." That finally worked.

As Connie stirred, she also awoke the man sleeping with her. In that same deep base voice I had heard this morning, he said, "Good morning Robert."

I instantly liked this man; he had a demeanor about him that I felt comfortable with. I asked, "Did you guys have fun last night?"

"Oh yes," Jeremy said, "Your wife is a wonderful lover."

I nodded, and watched Connie climbing out of bed. She was naked, but that wasn't much of a surprise. I patted her behind as she scrambled past me on her way to the bathroom.

Jeremy was also climbing out of bed, with every inch of his dark chocolate colored skin visible to me. I couldn't help but glance down at his cock, it looked to be adequate. I guessed that when erect, he might have measured out just over eight inches.

He walked towards me and extended his hand and we shook hands. I don't ever recall shaking a man's hand for the first time when he was in my bedroom, naked, not to mention black. A few moments later, Connie came out of the bathroom and asked if the coffee had been started yet. I told her no, that I had just awakened myself. She asked if I'd mind putting a rush on it.

I left the bedroom, wondering if they might try for a quickie but I assumed not when five minutes later, Jeremy wandered into the kitchen fully dressed. He informed me that Connie was in the shower.

That Friday, I had a morning meeting at one of our other offices at nine-thirty and I wasn't going to bother going to my desk first so I had some time that morning to spare. The coffee pot issued its final gurgling and I grabbed three cups from the pantry and poured coffee into them.

"Cream, Sugar?" I asked.

"Nah, black is fine." Jeremy said.

I fixed Connie's cup the way I knew she liked it and, trying to be a good host I suggested to Jeremy that he take it too her. He smiled at me and took her cup off the counter, carrying both his and hers back to the bedroom. He stopped however before entering the hallway and turned around.

"Robert, would you and Connie like to be my guest for dinner tonight?"

I said, "Sure, we'd love to."

Jeremy nodded and then turned back towards the hallway and disappeared. I thought that was nice of him. I took my cup into the living room. Since I had that extra time, I decided to stay out of the bedroom until after Connie finished getting dressed, assuming Jeremy allowed her to put clothes on. I was working up a fantasy whereby Jeremy talked Connie into calling in sick to work so they could spend the day fucking in my bed. I'd get home from work, then the three of us would all go out together to eat, a perfect day for all for sure.

I had just started my third and final cup of coffee when Jeremy rejoined me. He poured himself another cup and came over to sit on the sofa near my chair.

"I really like Connie," Jeremy began, "And I really want to thank you for allowing me to have access to her. You're a lucky man, and she's lucky to have an understanding husband."

I said, "Thank you," his manors impressed me. I think the thing that I liked is that he made it perfectly clear that he was *aware* that I was her husband while also being forthright about his interest in her. I just felt that it was such an honest approach.

He said he really appreciated any opportunity that he could have to date her and spend time with her. I told him about the white man Joey that Connie had dated for a few months so that he would see that this was something I was comfortable with. He continued to lavish compliments on both Connie and me as well.

A few moments later, Connie came out from the bedroom, dressed and ready for work. She leaned over, gave me a kiss on my cheek, and then gave Jeremy one as well telling him how much fun he had been to be with. Then she declared, "Robert, Jeremy is such a nice man, I just love him."

Okay, that was sort of uncomfortable, of course I knew what she meant but still, it kind of send a chill down my back. I've heard her say she liked someone many times but, well love is a four-letter word that, like others, needs to be used carefully. I dismissed it however, rather than say anything. I knew Connie really did like the man and enjoyed being with him, and that's all she really meant with her words.

It was getting close to eight and Connie needed to get going. Jeremy said he'd walk her to her car and then he needed to get on the road himself also, and that he would swing back by that evening to pick us up around six-thirty.

Alone now, I filled my cup for a fourth time and headed back to shower and get dressed. I was looking forward to dinner and hearing more about this new person in Connie's life, and interestingly enough, I was seeing this as a new person in our lives.

My meeting was boring and I couldn't focus too well on what was going on. I was reliving that moment when I first noticed the bed rocking the night before. It was such a bazaar and unexpected experience, perhaps like when you are way out in the country at night and by chance, a large meteor streaks across the sky. What I did notice during the meeting was how much of it was devoted to making an agenda for the next meeting.

There was a voice mail from Connie waiting for me when I finally got to my desk. I think she was having some fun with the idea that her and Jeremy had slide into bed with me during the night and fucked while I slept.

One of the first things you should jot down about your wife having a boyfriend is to note that a good one offers to pick up the dinner tab at least half the time. It also means that you get to go out to dinner twice as often, which is definitely a positive.

That evening, not only did Jeremy pick up the bill, which wasn't cheap either, he provided the transportation. Connie sat in front with her date while I stretched out in the back seat. One of the many fantasies I had envisioned occurred that night as I played the role of the friend to the happy couple. There was absolutely no doubt about which of us Connie was with that night. Her body language spoke volumes and Jeremy opened her door for her and walked hand-in-hand with her through the parking lot and into the restaurant.

Occasionally, I glanced around to see if other restaurant patrons were taking notice that a white woman was out with a black man, and I wondered if they speculated on the odds that she was getting big black cock off him.

My curiosity finally made me ask the question I had wanted to ask all day. "How come you guys came back to our place last night?"

Jeremy replied, "Well, my place doesn't have any furniture yet. It won't arrive for another week. All I have is an air mattress that I sleep on in the living room. And, your wife is too classy to take to a motel."

I saw Connie's eyes open wide and her jaw drop when she heard Jeremy's comment about her. I knew what was coming before she said it.

"Jeremy, why don't you stay with us until your furniture arrives? That air mattress, I'll bet your back is killing you in the morning."

"Well, I wouldn't want to impose," he said. Honestly, I truly believed that he was being sincere. Because of that, I joined in with Connie and urged him to stay adding, "It's just for a few days."

"It's settled then," said Connie, before Jeremy could say a word. He just nodded that yes, it was settled.

Of course, it was still way too early to classify Jeremy as Connie's boyfriend, however after nearly a week at our place, there definitely was a relationship happening.

That Friday evening, I brought up the issue of where everyone would be sleeping on the first official night he was living with us. Jeremy made his preferences clear to all of us. He told us that he thought it was cruel and unnecessary to keep a man out of his own bed.

I then suggested that he could make himself comfortable in the spare bedroom and of course; Connie was free to sleep wherever she wished. That night, that was how things went down. I took the king sized bed in the master bedroom and Connie and Jeremy snuggled together on the double in the guest bedroom. But, that only lasted one night. By Saturday night, all three of us were back in the master bedroom, with Connie snuggled in between us.

Saturday night was also the first time the three of us participated in a threesome and I think it went really well. My estimate on how long Jeremy's cock was however was a tad short. I realized after that first night that I usually needed to go first if I wanted to get some traction. Jeremy tended to pound on her quite a while and with his size, she was far too juicy inside for my taste afterwards.

By the fourth night, although I would continue to participate to a degree when it was Jeremy's turn, I usually rolled over and tried to get to sleep about halfway though their first session. They usually did it twice a night.

It was obvious that Connie enjoyed having Jeremy around the house, and he pitched in and did his part whenever he saw something that needed to be done. He even offered to mow the grass one day.

Thursday night, his eighth in our home, seventh as our roommate, he made the announcement over dinner that his furniture and belongings were finally arriving the next day. I could see the look in Connie's face.

I joked and said, "I'll bet you'll be glad to have a little privacy finally."

"No, I'll miss this woman of ours," he replied. He then added, "Robert, would you mind if Connie comes and stays with me for the weekend?"

I kind of knew I needed to say yes to his question, otherwise I'd appear as if I was jealous. I was of course, to a degree, but I trusted Connie, despite the fact that her eyes assured me that she wanted to 'move in' with Jeremy for the weekend. I told them I was okay with it.

Mentally, I was counting the nights that Connie had been with Jeremy and by the time this coming weekend was over, that would add up to about ten straight nights. The most consecutive nights she had ever slept with another man had been three up until then.

I also realized that the prophecy had come true after all. Although I don't think it had been intended, Connie had not gone back to white, except for me of course, since that first experience with Frank a couple of weeks ago, which now seemed almost an eternity.

If I worried at all, it was about what how Connie would handle the next week after she returned home. I decided to take advantage of having a free weekend and I decided to head over to the Indian Casino I'd wanted to visit that was located about fifty miles away. I ended up coming back about five hundred richer.

You should jot that down as another benefit of having a boyfriend for your wife so you can take off and do what you want occasionally. Not to mention that no one thought anything else but while Connie was his, he was responsible for her, feeding her, paying for those new shoes she couldn't live without. It adds up.

Any fears I had about that following Monday without Jeremy disappeared. Connie went out of her way to make my favorite dinner and we fucked in the living room on the couch that night. She went overboard to reassure me that *we* were still okay.

Jeremy did come back Wednesday night, but this time I insisted on picking up the dinner tab. And, paying for three instead of two isn't that much more anyway, and Jeremy drove.

I think he liked to be the chauffer, it made it more like a date for him and Connie and I enjoyed the role-play that went on as well. I wasn't surprised when Jeremy asked if Connie could come and stay the following weekend again.

I considered going back for another couple of nights to the casino but decided against it, it's nice to be ahead at a place, I wanted to stay that way for a while. I was just about ready to toss some hamburger meat into a frying pan Saturday night when the doorbell rang. It was Connie and Jeremy. They thought it was hilarious that they rang the bell, as guest, rather than just barging in. I thought it was funny too.

Well, they asked me if I wanted to go out for the evening, to a club and listen to music, dance a bit and I said that sounded great to me so they waited while I showered off and got dressed. That night, at the club, I came very close to picking up a woman and taking her home. None of us even hinted that Connie was my wife. In fact, I thought I heard the girl asking Connie how long she had been married to Jeremy.

Although the girl didn't work out for me that night, I think Connie was really pleased to see me reaching out to someone. I started to think that maybe, I should venture out a bit, maybe even develop my own girl friend scenario. Just needed to keep her away from big black cocks, that was one lessen I think I've

91

learned from this. Once they go black, its kind of hard to keep them focused; you know what I mean?

We stayed at the club until the band finished playing their final set. On the way back to my house, we stopped for a late snack/early breakfast at an IHOP. Connie and Jeremy dropped me off at home and then headed back over to Jeremy's apartment.

One of the main points I want to make is that during the week when Connie lived with me, she was ultra nice to me, going out of her way to see that I was a happy camper.

I think it was perhaps a month later when things changed a little. Instead of Connie shacking up at Jeremy's for the weekend, they decided to stay at our house instead. The weekend reminded all of us about how much we three enjoyed spending time together. That first evening, we sat around and played cards.

That night, when I think they thought I was asleep, I heard Jeremy whisper to Connie, "I love you," and I heard her respond back with, "I love you too, shush." I did not sleep much the rest of the night.

I guess I already knew that Connie and Jeremy were in love. The question was, what I should do about it. I was strangely unconcerned and I'm sure you're asking yourself, why wouldn't I be freaking out about this?

Did I want to lose Connie? Absolutely not, but I would be willing to share. You want to know what finally assured me that everything was going to be all right?

It was about two weeks later, a Wednesday night and Connie and I had just finished putting the dishes away, and I checked to see if we had any email on *SwingPartners*. There was an invitation to a party the following Saturday night. Of course, I knew Connie was spending the weekend at Jeremy's again, as usual and I suggested to her that maybe she and Jeremy could go to the party together. She loved the idea and said we three can all go together.

That's when I told her I had a date already, with a woman I'd met one weekend night two weeks before.

Loudly and with excitement, Connie screamed "What?"

"I said, I have a date Saturday. Her name is Trisha and we're going out to dinner and then to a movie."

"Why don't you bring her to the party?"

I considered the idea for a moment and said, "No, I don't think she's ready for something like that."

"Does she know you're married?"

"Yes," I said. I knew Connie was crazy with curiosity. I had some fun with her at first by revealing only minimal details however there really wasn't much to it yet.

"Have you guys fucked yet?"

"Oh yeah, I stayed at her apartment that first night I met her."

"Why didn't you tell me?" she asked.

"Honestly, I meant to as soon as you got home that first Monday when you got home but I just forgot about it."

"Robert," she scolded, "If you're going to be going out and getting strange pussy, you need to keep your wife informed! You should know that."

"Yes, I know… I'm sorry."

The real truth was, that I was waiting on just the right moment to tell Connie about Trisha. Having a scheduling conflict seemed to be the perfect moment and I was enjoying how the conversation was going.

One thing I really wanted to see was whether Connie was actually jealous. What I hoped was, that she could take it just as much as she could dish it out. Now, I don't mean that to mean I was getting even with her. What I was worried about was if she felt jealousy, she might also start feeling guilty about her relationship with Jeremy.

Of course I had occasional periods of loneliness when she in her lover's arms but our own times together seems so much better since she started splitting her time between us. I didn't want that to stop and I saw a distinct advantage to having my own little lady on the side to spend some time with occasionally. Did I mention that Trisha's a knockout and gives great head?

The following Monday, I ran into some traffic and was nearly an hour late getting home. Connie was nearly ready to serve dinner and had even started worrying about me. As soon as I walked in and she stopped kissing me, I asked, "How did the party go?"

"How did your date with Trisha go?" she said.

I said, "You first, but yes, Trisha and I had a great time. Your turn and I'll tell you more later after you tell me what happened at the party."

"Let me turn down the oven," she said.

A few minutes later, Connie and I were spread out on the couch, her bare feet in my lap being massaged.

"Well, at first, I didn't think I could get Jeremy to go to the party but finally, he said if I wanted to, he wanted to. So, we went. It was the first time he was ever at something like that and he kept asking me what to expect and whether there would be any other black people there. I told him there probably wouldn't be and that we've never seen any black or mixed couples there before.

Well, then he starts worrying that some of the other couples might not feel comfortable with a black man there and I told him that worst case, I'd fuck and suck him and have so much fun that every woman there would be after him. And, they were too. As soon as we walked in, he had two women hanging off his arm."

"So, he fucked other women?"

"Most of them I think," Connie said, laughing.

"What about you Sweetie? Did you get some strange dick?"

"Oh yes, let's see, Tim and Joanie were there, I did Tim and Bob and Francis, I didn't do Hank this time but I think I did at least six or seven guys, I lost count."

"Wow," I said, "you usually can't handle that many guys."

"Well, blame Jeremy for that, he's got me spoiled."

"I'll bet," I said.

"You know what I was thinking?" Connie said, "Well, Jeremy was so popular at that party, I wondered… what would it be like to go to a black swingers party, where I was the only white woman?"

"I suspect, in fact I'd even bet that you'd get fucked a lot." I said, "but, you know what? If I went with you, maybe I'd have plenty of brown sugar myself."

"I'll bet," Connie nodded.

So dear friend, I'm nearly done with my story, I had no idea I had so much to say about things. After listening to how well things had gone at the swinger's party, I asked Connie the hard questions.

"Do you think Jeremy was upset at all? Seeing you with other men?"

"Oh no, in fact he was on the same bed with me fucking some other woman when I was getting fucked and I heard him telling my guy to fuck me good because he was going to be worn out with the woman he was with."

"And, what about you? How did you feel about seeing Jeremy with another woman?"

"Didn't bother me, it was just fucking, why should it?"

"True," I said, "we're pretty far past being concerned about who fucks who."

"Ya think," Connie laughed.

"Seems so," I replied, "but, what about you and Jeremy?"

"I don't follow, what are you asking?"

I looked down at her feet and said, "I know you and Jeremy are lovers."

Connie paused for a moment before answering, "Yes... so?"

"Well, so... where does that leave us?"

"You're my husband Robert."

"Yes, but..."

"Yes, but nothing Honey, you are my husband and you always will be."

I looked up at Connie and asked, "So where does that leave Jeremy?"

"Jeremy is my lover, and probably always will be. Can't I have a lover and a husband? Can't I love both?"

"Yes you can," I said, "but CAN you?"

"I don't know," she said softly, "I think so and I hope so."

"Okay, so we just keep things the way they are?" I asked.

"Nope," Connie said, "I think we should do what Jeremy suggested."

"And, what did Jeremy suggest?"

"Jeremy said we should all live together… you, me, him… and who knows, maybe your new friend Trisha someday."

I looked at Connie, and I had tear running down my cheek. I said, "I think Jeremy had a great idea. I was going to suggest the same thing myself."

Well friend that is pretty much the entire story, the only other thing is that Connie called Jeremy and asked him to come over that evening. He ended up spending the night and we three played all night long together.

Jeremy moved in shortly after that but we couldn't really figure out how to make the finances work so Connie and I ended up selling a third of the house to Jeremy so that all expenses could be shared evenly. For the hell of it, Connie and Jeremy took a quick trip across the Mexican border and they got married. It wasn't legal of course, but regardless, it made us feel official.

Trisha didn't work out but I did find a Honey about a month after I broke up with Trisha. Do you remember Chantil? We heard that her and Dennis had a falling out about something and they weren't married in the first place. So, I suggested that she come and stay with us until she figured out what to do. She's still here and now that she is away from Dennis, she is a lot more like the woman I spent the night with than who she seemed to be with Dennis at her elbow.

What's really amusing is that when the four of us go out together, most people probably assume that it's Jeremy and Chantil together, and Connie and I together when actually, it tends to vary a little anytime the four of us go out.

Overall, I'm spending most nights with Chantil but the four of us swap off occasionally and sometimes it's a free for all in the big bed. We're talking about getting another house where the other bedrooms are a little larger, especially if Chantil decides to join the family on a permanent basis.

I suppose it isn't necessary for an open marriage to go as far as ours did, but without letting Connie get to that first base where she believed that she had a boyfriend, I doubt that things would have worked out as well as they have.

So friend, I'm not giving you advice but that's how it worked for us. I wish you and your wife a lot of luck and the fact that the man she ran off with last week is a well-endowed black man doesn't mean you are going to lose her forever. You just need to let her know, reassure her that you are okay with her having a black boyfriend and lover, and that you still love her too. If you two can agree to be open and honest, and willing to adjust to each other's needs, hopefully you can convince her and her black lover to come back to you.

Message me back if there is anything else I can help you with.

Best of luck,

Robert, Connie, Jeremy, and Chantil

About the Author

From *Simone and the Writer:* It occurred to him that perhaps, he might be a better writer of erotic fiction if he targeted his craft towards one person at a time, making love to one reader at a time.

*****

I.M. Telling lives in the southern United States, on the coast and has been a non-fiction writer for some time. He has always wanted to write erotica and is finally making that dream a reality. His writing includes everything from highly explicit erotica featuring interracial relationships, swinging, and cuckold tales to very sensual stories of bondage and examining the dynamics of open marriage. His writing has also started to extend into other genres including adventure, humor, and stories with extreme violence.

Telling states that he prefers to evolve the characters within his tales, making their journey from where they start to where they reach by the last page as the reason for the story.

"I am convinced that the mind is the most powerful sex organ in the body. I hope my stories generate stirrings within the reader, by being somewhat specific with the x-rated portions. Yet I mostly want my readers to make a journey of their own as they follow the changes happening inside the minds of my characters, who I consider to be my friends. I never judge nor fault my characters, as it is their journey and not necessarily mine."

I. M. Telling

Contact Information
email Address: LateNightPublishing@gmail.com
Twitter: https://twitter.com/#!/I_M_Telling
Authors' Web Site: http://www.LateNightPublishing.biz
Facebook:
http://www.facebook.com/#!/profile.php?id=10000378272236
0

Please feel free to send an email to I. M. Telling regarding his existing works plus any story ideas you might have.

*****

Visit I. M. Telling's Website:

http://www.LateNightPublishing.biz for inside the book previews as well as buy-links to major online resellers.

Edited by Lilith Kyper

If you are an author in search of reasonable editing and proofing services, write to her at lilithkypereditor@gmail.com

Bibliography

Being Serviced – Hard core interracial, where white women are given over by their husbands to big black monster cocks at a hotel floor takeover party.

Being Serviced by the Best – The sequel to Being Serviced where high profile black athletes assemble best-in- breed married white women for the ultimate party.

Brenda Bailey Cunningham's Ankle Bracelet – A tale of sexual obsession, dominance, and submission. A husband buys a birthday present for his wife that contains her initials (BBC). Neither the husband or the wife are aware of the meaning if this jeweler accessory in the cub-culture of interracial sex.

The Wager: Episode One of High Stakes Erotica - A young couple, Jack and Chloe, dare each about whether the wife will participate in a gangbang. Both the husband and wife are sure that their spouse will chicken out before it is too late.

Another Wager: Episode Two of High Stakes Erotica - After Chloe's hot night, she feels that it is hubby's night to play. She sends him out on his with strict orders to make a score.

Raising the Stakes: Episode Three of High Stakes Erotica - Tonight, Jack and Chloe will meet their first couple together, becoming full-fledged swingers.

Laying Odds: Episode Four of High Stakes Erotica - Jack and Chloe are ready for their first full-blown group orgy. Kinks neither of them knew they had are explored.

Black Jack: Episode Five of High Stakes Erotica - Their marriage is open now; Chloe takes a lover. Henry is an African American, and he increases many of Jack's wife's pleasures.

All In: Episode Six of High Stakes Erotica - The couple experiments with prostitution, as the Chloe becomes a paid escort. "After all," Jack says, "Why just give it away?"

Full House: Episode Seven of High Stakes Erotica - An experiment in polyamorous living as Chloe's lover moves in. But Jack's two lady friends want to join the household as well.

Hit Me: Episode Eight of High Stakes Erotica - Erotica. Dominance, submission, and other kinky fetishes from the world of BDSM are explored as Jack and Chloe visit a local dungeon for the first time.

Black Cock Lawyer – She terrorized white men by day, but her nights are reserved for the big black cocks she craves. Sheila is a slut beyond belief who brings home tasty treats for her unaware husband to enjoy.

High Stakes Erotica – The complete set of all eight stories that follows Jack and Chloe from their introduction into the world of swinging until they had experienced everything along their journey. (Paperback Only)

My Knees are Knocking but You Can't Come In… Yet! – Kissed at a party by her African American neighbor Darnel, a white wife decides she wants to play. However, it is Darnel's Hispanic wife Lucinda who comes calling.

The Burglar's Surprise – A burglar, turned serial rapist, picks the wrong victim. It is a mistake he wished he had not made. Contains violent content.

Mari – An adventure tale of a woman who is seduced into a life of bondage and slavery. Does she have what it takes to extract bloody revenge from her tormentors?

Indica – A BDSM fetish tale of rope bondage and submission. Indica feels it is time to kick things up a notch.

Suzanne – Exclusive to black men, and proud and content with her life, a white woman finally finds happiness.

Willy and the Couple – Widowed two years earlier, Willy decides to finally experience his ultimate fantasy. All his life, he has fantasized about being with a white woman.

I'm Telling Quickies: Volume One – Sometimes, all you need is a quickie. I. M. Telling has six maniacal and twisted sex stories to fill your needs.

Simone and the Writer – A woman in a marriage gone wrong finds excitement in explicit writings about interracial sex. She makes contact with the writer whose words take her to the next level and far beyond.

Ebony Knights and Ivory Ladies – A group of well-endowed ebony studs entertain a group of ivory toned couples at monthly parties, the fun begins when one of the ivory wives desires to be ebony bred.

Getting Even in Unexpected Ways – Patricia knew she had to get out of the house that morning; otherwise, her anger at her philandering husband would drive her insane.

Bob for Christmas – A short story for Christmas time about a woman who wants to help her daughter grow into a woman, while avoiding the mistakes her own mother made.

Big Black Cock – Alex lived in a world where he thought he was the master of all he surveyed as women threw themselves on their knees before him. One night, he witnessed a reflection of what he had become and he didn't like what he saw.

In Serious Need of a Big Black Cock – Sometimes you have an itch and you need to get it scratched, probed, played with, and stimulated and there is only one thing that will provide it to you.

Filming in Color - Jeannie had yet to experience her first on-screen kiss but the role required far more than just kissing a man. The part required full nudity and included an explicit sexual encounter with an African American. Raised in a conservative environment that was prejudicial towards blacks, this would also be the challenge of a lifetime.

The Zebra Lounge – The right set of six lottery numbers opened many doors for Mark and Marlene. Mark was finally able to make his dream of an interracial club a reality. His goal was to supply as much big black cock to white pussies as possible. Erotica writer Long John O'Tool brings his woman to sample the offerings at *The Zebra Lounge*.

The Zebra Lounge Revisited – Erotica author Long John O'Tool and his companion Carla return to The Zebra Lounge the following night. It's another wild night for them both. Long John hears stories about the clubs opening night and Coach gives Carla everything she desires and more.

The Confession – A jaded woman thinks she is hard core, until her shy friend brings her up to date with her recent experiences. The Confession is an outlandish story that will make you laugh or cringe.

Dear John – No one likes getting a '*Dear John*' letter from a wife or girl friend. If you have received one, hopefully it was not like this one; total satire from the twisted mind of I. M. Telling.

Dear Jane – No one likes getting a Dear John or a Dear Jane letter, but sometimes, a woman is better off when her man leaves her. This is another twisted satire from I. M. Telling's warped mind.

The Ebony Letter – The making of an interracial cuckold is explored in detail. It begins with an average Joe finds a journal written by a couple immersed into the work of interracial swinging.

Cuck'd – A dark, highly explicit tale about a couple named Doug and Serena. Serena's fascination with being an exhibitionist leads the couple into a world of interracial sex and cuckoldry. Dragged into a world that he never truly wanted, Doug finds himself strangely attracted to aspects of his new life.

The Complete Asshole's Guide to Getting Laid Online – Everyone needs to score some strange ass occasionally. Online fuck sites make it a breeze to connect to like-minded people. Just make sure you are not an asshole.

My Wife's Black Boyfriend – Robert and Connie take their marriage far beyond just swapping with other couples and enjoying the occasional orgy. Sometimes, things get serious when people start having sex with others.

CPSIA information can be obtained at www.ICGtesting.com
Printed in the USA
LVOW07s2018040116

469060LV00025B/1429/P

9 781482 631647